THE NEXT FILES
DOUBLE PUZZLER

EIGHT DRAGONS

and

THE MIN MIN

by

G. L. Keady

ALSO BY
G. L. Keady

DREAMRAIDERS
SONS OF STEEL
CHANNELING BO
THE INCARNATE

Axis Stone Mysteries Series

SUICIDE BLONDE
LEG MAN
SMUGGLER'S HOLE
HORSE ARM CASE
GOD'S DOOR
THE SACRED THREE
THE GIRL WITH THE LUNATIC FRINGE
CAT STREET
THE ZIGGY STARDUST DEAD RINGER

The Sons of Steel Saga

FUTURES END
CYBERWARS
DARK ENERGY
BLOCKCHAIN
AL AND THE ID
TABLETS OF DESTINIES
DOMINION
ALL THE TIME IN THE WORLD

Published in Australia in 2024
by Big Island Publishing

Copyright © Gary Keady 2024

The right of Gary Keady to be identified as the moral rights
author of this work has been asserted by him in accordance
with the *Copyright Amendment (Moral Rights) AD. 2000*

This book is copyright.

Apart from any fair dealing for the purposes of private study,
research, criticism or review, as permitted under the Copyright Act,
no part may be reproduced by any process without written permission.
Enquiries should be addressed to the publishers.

All rights reserved.

No portion of this work may be copied by any means without
prior written agreement of the publishers.

Big Island Publishing
PO Box 3027, Tuross Head, 2537, NSW, Australia.
www.bigislandpublishing.au

ISBN:
E-book: 9780975633045
Print: 9780975633052

Edited by: Canon Doyle
Cover design and art: Brandon Evans-Keady

TABLE OF CONTENTS

CHAPTER ONE

It was closing time at the Eight Dragons restaurant in Sydney's Chinatown. The night had been busy, but for the staff, the work was far from over. As the last customer left and the front doors were locked, the large restaurant buzzed into clean-up mode. Tables were stripped of their cloths, vacuums roared to life on the backs of the cleaning crew, a stark contrast to the tranquil dining atmosphere patrons had enjoyed. This whirlwind of activity was orchestrated by Mr Lao, the hands-on owner of the Eight Dragons. With thirty years of experience and having grown up in the family business, now in its fifth generation of Lao ownership, he was a seasoned restaurateur.

The kitchen was even more chaotic, with staff washing dishes, cleaning surfaces, organising utensils and condiments, and preparing for the next day's lunch rush.

As midnight approached, the staff gradually departed, leaving behind two junior kitchen hands still polishing the stainless-steel cooking equipment. Mr Lao switched off the lights in the dining area, gave the boys a nod to indicate his departure, and left them to finish. A night patrol security guard would wait for them to lock up.

It was only the second night on the job for the teenage boys. Following the executive chef's specific instructions, they worked alone. One of the boys, glancing at his checklist, retrieved a marked container from a large refrigerator. Inside were an apple, an apricot, a peach, four ripe strawberries, and half a dozen lychees. He carried the container to a sink, where a twelve-centimetre tube descended through the floor. It seemed ancient, as if it had been there for a century. His task was to pour the contents into the tube, but deeming it wasteful, he covertly transferred the fruit to his bag.

Meanwhile, the other boy mopping the floor suddenly felt a chill. The dim lighting and eerie quietude were unsettling enough, but this cold sensation heightened his anxiety. He considered if it was the open refrigerator or perhaps the air conditioning. Resuming his mopping, he was startled when something gripped the mop. Paralysed, he released it, and it remained upright, seemingly defying gravity. Panicked, he called out, "Dixon, Dixon, come here ... quick!"

Dixon sauntered over, only to be amused at the sight. Grabbing the mop, he found himself in a tug-of-war with an unseen force. He struggled, but the mop was immovable, as if cemented to the floor. Abruptly, it jerked free and moved autonomously. Kitchen items started to shake and rattle, as if in the grip of an earthquake. A glass catapulted off a counter, shattering against the refrigerator. Pots and pans swung wildly, their clanging filling the air.

In a frenzy, Dixon yelled for the security guard, "Rick! Rick! Help!"

The guard burst in, halting abruptly at the chaos. The burly Pacific Islander exclaimed, "What the?" He ducked just in time as a meat cleaver whizzed past, embedding itself into the wooden door frame with a loud 'Thwack!' beside his ear. Wide-eyed, he shouted, "Get out of here, boys!"

They bolted for the exit, fluorescent lights bursting overhead, showering them with glass. Reaching the front door, the supernatural tumult ceased as abruptly as it had begun. Gasping for breath, hearts racing, they looked back into the darkened restaurant, bewildered and terrified by the unexplainable events they had just endured.

The Sydney production offices of 'NewsLine', a bustling daily television current affairs program, were a hub of activity. The open-plan workspace, home to the production staff, was dotted with a dozen cubicles, each equipped with a computer terminal. In contrast, senior executives had their own private offices.

It was mid-morning, and the office resembled a beehive: phones rang incessantly, and conversations crisscrossed the room. In one of the cubicles sat Jax de Loite, fresh out of school and new to the production team. Unlike her busy colleagues, she sat motionless, her expression one of boredom, which somewhat diminished her otherwise attractive appearance. In the cubicle next to hers, a pretty girl chewing gum stood up and peered over the partition at Jax.

"Hey Jax, you look bored to death," she remarked.

"You got that right, Meg. I finished today's work yesterday."

"You should learn to slow down like the rest of us, babe."

Meg walked away, passing Tilly, a big Filipino woman pushing a beverage trolley. Tilly stopped at Jax's cubicle, offering a big, knowing smile.

"Morning, Jax. Dear, if that face of yours gets any longer, your chin will hit the ground. How about a cup of tea?"

Jax returned the smile. "Thanks, Tilly."

Handing her a cup, Tilly whispered, "If I were you, I'd march right into his majesty's office over there and demand an assignment. You can do it."

Jax sipped her tea. "I guess ... but he only gave me the job because he knew dad. I'm only a research assistant, Tilly. I can't very well ask him for an assignment ... not yet."

Tilly, about to move off, paused. "Nonsense. You won't know till you try. Ask and you shall receive ... don't ask and you get nothing ... Well, you know what I mean ... it goes something like that..."

They shared a giggle, and Tilly gave her a big wink before moving off to serve another cubicle. Jax leaned back, chewing the end of her pen, her expression reflecting her growing courage. She got up and peered over her cubicle partition at the Producer's office. The job title on his door seemed foreboding. She murmured to herself, "You're so right, Tilly ... I am better than this."

Bolstered by newfound confidence, Jax marched down the corridor towards the Producer's office. She was acutely aware of her colleagues' and Tilly's eyes on her. Raising her fist to knock, she hesitated, hearing Des Carter's voice from inside, berating someone.

"You were at the network meeting yesterday ... you heard that if we don't come up with something hot to lift our ratings, it'll be all over for us ... So what do you give me? ... some cheesy story ... the same old rubbish you're all consistently churning out..."

Before Jax could retreat, the door swung open, revealing the fifties-plus Des Carter. Jax froze.

"Miss de Loite?" Carter questioned, surprised to see her standing there.

Flustered, senior line producer Janet Holmes stormed out of the office.

"And Janet," Carter called after her, causing her to pause and look back with a scowl. "Remind the senior producers... there are plenty of eager young reporters like this one here, ready to take their places."

Janet's scornful glance fell on Jax before she left.

Carter's attention returned to Jax. "So, Miss de Loite, can I help you?"

Jax, gathering her wits, stammered, "No sir ... I mean, yes, Mr Carter."

"I'll take that as a yes," Carter said, checking his watch. "I've got a meeting... you have a minute, come in."

Stepping into the office, Jax felt her nervousness intensify. The room was lined with TV Week Logie awards and various accolades, a testament to Carter's achievements. She suddenly doubted her resolve.

Carter sat down and twirled a pen. Despite his stern appearance, he exuded a natural charm. Clearly in a hurry, he urged, "Okay, okay, what's up? You seem intimidated."

"It's just ... all your achievements, sir. They sort of put you on a different level."

"Well, you might be a young woman, but you're certainly your father's daughter. He would've made the same observation, never afraid to voice his opinions ... always fought for the underdog ... something greatly lacking around here."

"Yeah, and going out there was what got him killed, trying to tell the underdog's story."

Carter's mood shifted at the reminder. "He's sadly missed ... A top-notch reporter ... but we move on. Now, what's on your mind?" The phone rang. "Hold that thought." Answering, he said, "Yes, I'm bloody late! Keep your shirt on, I'll be there soon." He hung up abruptly. "Bloody meetings ... How can I get anything done with constant departmental meetings?"

Jax took a deep breath. "Mr Carter, I know I can be a good reporter, but as a research assistant, I'm just being wasted."

"Okay ... I get that, I know it's in your blood ... Your father, his father before him, all incredibly talented journalists, but—"

She interrupted, "All men, as you said. Is it because I'm a woman or that I'm Koori that's stopping—"

"No, no, don't put words in my mouth. I was about to say ... they all had to start somewhere ... Christ, you've been here only three months and you're what, nineteen?"

"Almost nineteen, sir."

Carter stood up, indicating the meeting was over. "You should be at university..."

Jax stood up to leave. "No need for Uni. My dad trained me; I grew up in this game. I just want a chance to prove myself. You, more than anyone, should understand that. If I don't have what it takes, I'll go to Uni."

Carter tapped his desk with his forefinger, deep in thought. He sighed, and headed towards the door, then stopped and looked back at her. "Well, come on then. You might be just what we need."

Jax hurried after him, catching up as they strode down the corridor. Their movement drew curious glances from workstations along the way. Tilly, watching the scene unfold, gave Jax a knowing smirk and a thumbs-up behind Carter's back.

As they walked, Carter explained in a hurry, "Ever since the success of 'The X-Files' ages ago, every eccentric in Australia and the region has been sending us reports of UFO sightings, Bigfoot, ghosts, alien abductions, monsters—you name it, they've sent it. Occasionally, and I stress the word 'occasionally', one of these stories might have some substance, but after wasting buckets of money and valuable time on a crew and producer to check out a few credible leads, we just got fed up. They ended up here." He stopped at a door, opened it to reveal a small room crammed with boxes. "We call it 'The Next Files'. Out of sight, out of mind, but still updated regularly." He glanced at her, noticing the spark of excitement in her eyes. "Okay, you've got a shot. A minimal budget, no assistant, you're on your own in an office so small you can't swing a cat. Deliver one credible three-minute story a month. Up for it?"

Jax, in disbelief, stared wide-eyed at him, then back at the files, then back to him again. She was about to burst with excitement. "Mine? You're serious?"

"Your dad was a mate. He was the best, and you damn well remind me of him. As crazy as it sounds, 'The Next Files' are yours. Just don't let me down, de Loite."

Overcome with emotion, Jax embraced him with all the enthusiasm of a teenager receiving her first car.

It had been an extraordinary day for Jax, surpassing even her wildest dreams. The chance to delve into the realm of the unexplainable was a trait deeply ingrained in her family, a core part of the investigative spirit she had inherited from her parents. 'The Next Files' offered her much more than a mere challenge; it was a gateway to exploring the supernatural, the unbelievable, and the world of conspiracies—subjects that had always topped her list of interests.

CHAPTER
TWO

The production office was eerily quiet, illuminated by only minimal lighting. As Tilly was leaving for the day, she noticed light seeping out from under a door in the corridor. Curious, she realised Jax was still working long after everyone else had left. A temporary sign on the door read 'The Path.' Pushing the door open, Tilly found herself in a small, chaotically cluttered office, with stacks of boxes scattered everywhere.

"Are you in here somewhere, Jax?"

Jax peeked around a pile of boxes. "Oh, hi Tilly."

"My goodness, girl, all this paper ... You've got what's left of half the world's forests in here!"

Jax chuckled as she stood up. "These, Tilly, are the Next Files. Some of the most amazing stories you could ever imagine ... and my little office is the path to solving them."

"You've lost me, girl ... What are The Next Files?"

"It's thousands of unexplained incidents reported from all over Australia, New Zealand, and Southeast Asia ... years of them. Everything from UAPs to ghosts and monsters ... it's all here, real accounts but destined to be forgotten ... until now."

"Well, that should keep you busy. Why the rattled look?"

Jax opened her laptop and showed it to Tilly. "Despite all this, I've just been tasked with interviewing a Feng Shui master arriving from China tomorrow."

"So? Isn't that what you wanted?"

"I don't know the first thing about Feng Shui or Chinese culture. I need help, Tilly!"

Tilly paused, then said, "Go to the Friend in Hand Pub tonight at nine. Look for a man named Doc."

"Doc? Who's he?"

"He's a friend. A scientist, I think. He'll help you. I'll let him know you're coming. See, you ask, you get. Good, huh? Catch you later." Tilly left the room.

Left alone, Jax muttered to herself, "Doc, a scientist? At this rate, I'll end up as nuts as the other producers." She glanced around at the towering stacks of files. "I might have bitten off more than I can chew."

Later that evening, at nine, Jax arrived at the Friend in Hand Pub's main bar. The place wasn't packed; only about a dozen patrons were gathered near the dartboard. She scanned the room for someone who might be a doctor, but no-one fit the bill, so she headed to the bar.

"What'll it be, love?" the bartender asked.

"A middy of old, thanks. Do you know a guy named Doc?"

As the bartender pulled her beer, he replied with a smile, "Doc? Yeah, he's practically a fixture here. Over there, playing darts."

"Thanks," Jax said, taking her beer and paying.

She took a sip and walked towards the group at the dartboard. Jax observed a man with his back to her, his dart throw hitting the bullseye with impressive precision, securing the game. The group erupted in cheers and pats on his back. Uncertain of which one was Doc, Jax approached the most scholarly-looking guy in the group, who wore glasses and a corduroy jacket, and had the 'nerd' appearance of a scientist. He was applauding the winner. "Nice shooting, mate," he said to the dart champion.

The winner, dressed in biker gear and of Asian descent, responded, "You owe me a pig's ear."

"Excuse me, are you Doc?" Jax asked tentatively.

The biker turned to face her, and their eyes met in a moment of mutual surprise.

"Yes, there is a doctor in the house ... so it must be me. You must be Jax de Loite ... I didn't know you were..."

"Aboriginal ... And I didn't realise you were..."

"Australian ... well, Asian by pedigree," he joked with a light tone.

Jax was momentarily taken aback; he didn't at all fit her image of a scientist. He was about her age or slightly older, with longish brown hair, tall, and had a rebel-like allure. He could easily be mistaken for a rock star.

"You throw a mean dart for a scientist," Jax remarked.

"It's all in the science of it ... the way you hold your mouth when you throw," he replied with a hint of humour.

Jax, caught off guard by his response, then realised he was joking and smiled.

"Tilly said you might need some help," he said. "Let's find a quieter spot."

He led them to a table in a more secluded part of the pub.

"Yeah ... Look, I don't know if you can but ... Um, I have a segment to write..."

Before she could continue, Matt approached with a beer for Doc and said, "Paid in full. Cheers."

"Ta, Matt. Cheers," Doc said, accepting the beer and taking a sip. He then turned back to Jax. "Tilly told me a bit about what you do ... Sounds interesting ... but how can I help?"

Jax hesitated. "I have to interview a Feng Shui master arriving from China tomorrow. He's quite famous, but I don't know the first thing about Feng Shui. Do you?"

"No, not my scene. Feng Shui is more about superstition than science," Doc admitted.

"Oh, I see."

Doc stood up, ready to leave. "Sorry, I don't think I can be of help there." He raised his glass in a toast and started to walk away.

Jax, struck by a sudden thought, called after him. "Doc, wait!"

He stopped and turned back, only a few steps away.

"Do you speak Chinese?" Jax asked.

Doc walked back towards her, beer in hand. "Mandarin or Cantonese?"

"I'm not sure ... Does it make a difference?"

"Absolutely. Mandarin is mostly spoken in northern China, Cantonese in the south. They're completely different."

"Which one do you speak?"

"A bit of both. Mandarin mostly, but not fluently."

Jax looked puzzled. "Not fluently?"

"It's like asking if you speak Wiradhuri."

"What's Wiradhuri?"

"The language of the Wiradhuri tribe from the Sydney area in 1788."

Jax scrunched up her nose and said, "Don't be ridiculous."

"Exactly. I'm an Aussie. We don't always fit the stereotype, do we?"

Jax chuckled, acknowledging his point, and raised her glass. "Touché. I'll drink to that. Peace?"

"Peace," Doc agreed, smiling. "And just for the record, I'm not a scientist yet. Still finishing up Uni."

They clinked glasses and sipped their beers.

Jax took a chance. "Would you come with me tomorrow to meet the Feng Shui master?"

Doc's expression brightened for a moment, then he shook his head, signalling a 'no', and began to walk away.

Disheartened, Jax put down her glass and got up to leave. Just then, Doc called out from a distance, "What time, and where?"

CHAPTER THREE

oc parked his black Harley Davidson Heritage Classic in a no-standing zone outside the Eight Dragons Restaurant in Sydney's Chinatown. Almost immediately, a parking cop approached him.

"No parking here. Move it, or I'll give you a ticket," the officer warned.

Stepping off his bike, Doc reached into his leather jacket, quickly pulled out his wallet, flashed his ID too fast for her to read, and said, "Move on, or your attitude will buy you early retirement." Without waiting for a response, he headed into the restaurant.

Inside, in a private room, Jax sat at a table with Feng Shui master Xiang Zi, nervously checking the time. Doc was running late. The old man poured her tea.

Jax spoke slowly and deliberately, "Thank - you. So - sorry. My - friend - who - speaks – your language - will - be - here - soon."

"No problem, we can speak in..." Xiang began.

Before Jax could fully grasp that Xiang was speaking English, she spotted Doc and quickly stood up. "Finally..."

Doc, helmet under his arm, took a seat. "Sorry I'm a bit late."

"More like three-quarters of an hour late," Jax retorted with a hint of cynicism.

Doc nodded respectfully to Xiang. "Nǐ hǎo."

Xiang replied in Mandarin, "I've been trying to explain to your friend that I speak very good English. But she seemed insistent on waiting for you to speak Mandarin."

"I see. I'm Vincent Lee, but everyone calls me Doc. Let's continue in Mandarin, to make her happy," Doc suggested.

"My name is Xiang Zi," the master replied.

They both turned to look at Jax, who seemed pleased they were conversing in their native tongue.

"Doc, could you ask Mr Zi if the Feng Shui is good in this restaurant?" Jax requested.

Doc smiled and translated in English, "Mr Zi, Jax wants to know if the Feng Shui here is good."

Despite Doc merely translating her question, Jax waited anxiously for Xiang's response.

"Yes," Xiang replied in English, "The Feng Shui is good, but there is some disturbance."

Jax looked puzzled, unsure if she had heard correctly.

Doc began to explain, "He said—"

Jax quickly realised her mistake. "Oh, I heard! I'm sorry, Mr Zi, I didn't realise you speak English so well. Please accept my apology."

"No problem, Jax. Always remember to ask and you will receive ... or something like that," Xiang said with a chuckle.

They all laughed. Jax frowned slightly, the phrase sounding familiar. She then took out her phone and switched it to record mode.

"So, Mr Xiang Zi, can you actually see spirits?"

"Yes. Everybody has spirits hanging from their backs. Mostly they are good spirits, but sometimes they are bad. You have the ability to see them as well, Jax, but you need to exercise the spiritual abilities you have inherited. You, on the other hand, my boy, are a total sceptic."

Doc grinned, "So, how many spirits are hanging off me, Xiang?"

Suddenly, a look of abject horror crossed Xiang's face, his gaze fixed on something unseen by Jax and Doc. He clutched at his chest, overcome by what seemed like excruciating pain. Attempting to rise to his feet, he struggled for a moment before collapsing onto the floor, apparently in the throes of a heart attack. Waiters from the establishment, alerted by the commotion, rushed towards the scene.

Later that evening, Jax was nervously pacing the hospital corridor, biting her knuckle. Doc casually strolled up to her, sipping a coffee and holding another one in his hand for her. He offered it to her.

"Here you go. Got time to drink it?"

"What?" she replied, perplexed.

"Well, you're obviously trying to wear a trench in the floor. The coffee means you'll at least have to stop your pacing for a moment to take a sip."

"Don't be ridiculous ... The caffeine will make me pace faster," Jax retorted.

He chuckled. "Let's sit down and..."

Before Doc could finish, a nurse interrupted them.

"Friends of Mr Zi? He's asking for you."

She led them along the corridor.

"Was it a heart attack?" Doc inquired.

"We think so, but some of the normal post symptoms are missing ... and that has the doctor a little confused," the nurse replied.

They entered the room where Xiang Zi was lying unconscious, connected to various machines. The digital beeps and blurts from the equipment unnerved Jax. She moved to his bedside, while Doc continued his conversation with the nurse.

"Such as what?"

"Well, for one, after a heart attack the patient's blood pressure would be expected to be either too high or too low, but Mr Zi's is normal."

"So what does that tell you?"

"It might not have been a heart attack? Excuse me," she said, leaving the room.

Doc watched her leave, and Jax noticed.

"Is any female safe around you?"

"Not if she's wearing a uniform," he quipped.

Just then, Xiang Zi opened his eyes. Doc sat on the other side of the bed from Jax, who took Xiang's hand.

"Hello to both of you. Ah, what an experience. I need to check out of here," Xiang said.

"Oh no, you don't. You had a heart attack," Jax responded quickly.

"I had no such thing," Xiang insisted.

Doc interjected, "Pardon me, but how else can you explain what happened?"

The old man struggled to sit up, and Jax quickly assisted him.

"It was an evil spirit," Xiang declared.

"A ghost?" Jax asked, incredulously.

Doc shook his head dismissively. "Yeah, right, in your dreams."

Xiang became agitated. "It came into the restaurant, saw me, and rushed at me ... It reached into my chest, grabbed my heart, trying to stop it beating. It wanted to kill me!"

His excitement caused the blood pressure machine to start beeping urgently.

"Easy, old man, settle down or you'll blow a fuse," Doc cautioned.

Ignoring him, Xiang started pulling off the sensors, causing the medical equipment to go haywire.

The nurse hurried into the room amidst the chaos and said in fluster, "You two need to leave. I have to sedate him."

As Doc stood up to leave, Xiang grabbed his arm. Speaking earnestly in Mandarin, he implored, "Listen, son, and believe me. I am in great danger. If I am sedated, I cannot protect myself from the evil spirit. Fetch my daughter Yan from the hotel. She is my apprentice; she will know what to do."

After the nurse administered the sedative, Xiang drifted off to sleep.

"What did he say?" Jax asked as they left the room.

Once outside, Doc spoke in hushed tones. "He wants his daughter, Yan, with him."

"Is that all? He seemed way too intense for just that. You're holding something back, Doc."

"He's a sick old man, Jax, maybe even delusional..."

Jax folded her arms, demanding the truth. "Doc?"

"Okay ... okay ... he thinks the evil ghost might get him while he's defenceless ... sedated ... His daughter is his apprentice ... he reckons she'll know what to do."

Without hesitation, Jax dashed down the corridor. "Stay here, Romeo. I'll fetch her from the hotel."

Doc shook his head and muttered, "Romeo, huh?" His attention was quickly diverted by a pretty nurse passing by.

CHAPTER
FOUR

Jax, stuck in peak hour traffic, called Xiang's hotel and was connected to Yan's room. "Hi, Yan ... I'm Jax, the one who interviewed your father ... Yes, he said it was an evil spirit and that you'd know what to do ... Your cell number? 77888 ... Got it. Okay, I'll be there in five or so. Bye."

Jax sat in her car outside the Observatory Hotel, frequently glancing at her watch in impatience. The only people in sight were a doorman, an elderly couple, and a stunning Chinese girl in tight jeans and a midriff top, a duffel bag slung over her shoulder, looking like a model on her way to or from a job.

"Damn ... where is she?" Jax muttered to herself.

She dialled Yan's number while observing the hotel entrance. The beautiful Chinese girl outside answered her phone.

"Yan?" Jax suddenly realised the model-looking girl was Yan. "Is that you? Okay."

Yan opened the car door and hopped in, extending her hand. "Hi, I'm Yan."

Jax, taken aback, stammered, "I didn't think ... that ... I mean, I sort of expected ... Oh, forget it. I'm Jax, of course. Got everything you need?"

Yan handed her a slip of paper. "No ... we have a little shopping to do."

"Okay ... where to, Chinatown?" Jax asked, expecting to head somewhere for exotic Asian supplies.

"No, just any hardware store," Yan replied.

Jax was surprised, having anticipated a more mystical list of items. "Oh. Okay," she said.

While driving, Jax stole a few discreet glances at Yan, attempting to figure her out. She finally broke the silence, "Do you live in China?"

"No, San Francisco. Pop's getting older, so he's been teaching me the trade."

"Feng Shui?"

"It's more than just Feng Shui. Pop is a Fashi, and it's a tradition that dates back to ancient China in our family. Feng Shui is about harmonizing people with their environment, but Fashi are experts in Daoist rituals and practices. They combat evil spirits and restore balance, using talismans, spells, and enchanted weapons in their supernatural battles."

"So, the tools we're getting from the hardware store are to fight a ghost?" Jax asked, trying to grasp the concept.

"Exactly," Yan confirmed.

Doc, immersed in a book on forensic DNA testing, looked up just as Jax and Yan approached Xiang's hospital room. He quickly stood up upon noticing Yan's striking appearance.

Jax, well aware of Doc's tendencies, quipped, "Easy, Doc ... This is Yan, Xiang's daughter."

Doc, trying to maintain composure, greeted her. "Unbelievable ... I mean, pleased to meet you. I'm Doc."

Yan smiled at him. "Hi ... Jax has told me quite a bit about you."

Doc glanced at Jax sceptically. "Don't believe everything she says. She tends to exaggerate."

"Told you so," Jax said, sharing a knowing smirk with Yan.

They entered Xiang's room, where he lay asleep amidst the humming and beeping of machines. Yan quickly got to work, pulling out a mirror and other items from her duffel bag and lighting incense sticks around the bed.

"There's no real danger of the ghost coming here," she assured them.

The nurse walked in, taken aback by the scene. "What are you doing? Burning incense? That's not permitted here."

Yan calmly explained, "It's to protect my father."

The nurse acquiesced slightly. "No incense and definitely no chanting."

"No incense, no chanting," Yan agreed.

Jax and Doc echoed, "No chanting."

After the nurse left, Doc commented sarcastically, "What's next, do we sacrifice a chicken or sing nursery rhymes backwards?"

Yan shot back, "I don't think your friend here has much faith in us, Jax."

Jax replied, "Ignore him. He's more into beer, motorbikes, and darts."

"Speaking of darts..." Doc began, but was interrupted by the entrance of two middle-aged Chinese businessmen.

"Good evening. I am Mr Wang, and this is Mr Chow. We represent the Chinatown Business Association. We brought Mr Xiang Zi here to Australia and would like to discuss his recent experience," Mr Wang said.

Jax indicated the sleeping Xiang. "He can't talk right now, but this is his daughter, Yan."

"May we speak privately, Miss Zi?" Mr Wang asked.

"No need. Speak freely," Yan invited.

The businessmen looked slightly uncomfortable but proceeded.

"We've heard Mr Zi believes an evil spirit attacked him," Mr Wang said.

"Yes, that's correct," Yan confirmed.

Jax added, "It tried to kill him."

Doc, ever the sceptic, interjected, "Let's not jump to conclusions without evidence."

Mr. Chow spoke up, "Needless to say, if this was to be made public, it would be very bad for Chinatown business."

Unexpectedly, Xiang spoke up, "For how long have you been hiding the truth?"

"Papa!" Yan exclaimed happily, taking Xiang's hand.

Wang and Chow approached Xiang, bowing to him, and Wang spoke in Mandarin.

"We honour you, Master Xiang Zi, and we ask for your assistance in this matter."

"Please speak in English so my friend Jax can understand," Xiang requested.

Jax felt honoured by his consideration.

"So sorry, Miss Jax. We are asking for Master Xiang Zi to help us," Wang translated.

Xiang glared at the two businessmen. "I asked how long have you concealed the truth about the ghost?"

"The ghost has been there as long as Chinatown," Chow admitted.

"Maybe even longer," Wang added.

Doc was sceptical. "Come on, really?"

Chow continued, "The ghost has only broken items and scared staff over the years. It has remained under control because we have left offerings to it."

Wang added, "The offerings keep it at bay."

"But now the ghost is angry because it has been seen," Xiang stated.

"Yes. Tonight it smashed many things in the Eight Dragons restaurant ... two large fish tanks, plates, bottles..." Wang said.

"It caused a lot of damage and frightened off the customers," Chow added worriedly. "Can you rid us of the ghost, the cost matters not?"

"Jax, can I have a word with you outside?" Doc asked.

"Sure. Excuse us."

Outside, Doc spoke. "It's a scam."

"What are you talking about?"

"It's a total setup. Xiang and his daughter Yan cruise around all the Chinatowns in the world, frightening the crap out of the superstitious Chinese business community. All to get paid heaps to get rid of a ghost that doesn't even exist. The perfect scam. Don't you see?"

Jax thought for a moment, then said, "Hmm, you might have a point."

"You watch. It's all about the money ... I know the Chinese, Jax."

Jax was nodding her head, almost convinced by Doc's theory, when Yan emerged from Xiang's room and said, "Excuse me, Jax, I need to ask you something."

"Sure, Yan, go ahead."

"Well, father is not in any condition to exorcise the ghost, so I'm going to have to do it ... but I will need some help. Can I rely on you guys?"

Doc was just about to respond when Wang and Chow exited the room.

"We thank you so much, Miss Zi," Wang said. "We will make preparations for you to enter the restaurant tonight."

Chow looked concerned. "Are you certain you will not accept any payment?"

"Yes, I am certain of this, Mr Chow. It is not our policy to make money from the problems of people."

Jax raised an eyebrow at Doc and whispered to him, "So you know Chinese, huh? From what, Jackie Chan movies?"

"We thank you, Miss Jax and Doctor Lee," Wang said graciously.

"Yeah," Doc replied casually. "Glad we could be of help."

Jax muttered under her breath to Doc, "Hypocrite."

Yan then asked, "So, will you help me tonight?"

CHAPTER FIVE

At 2 am, Chinatown resembled a ghost town. Eerie tendrils of winter mist drifted through the silent streets. A solitary rat scuttled across the footpath, its movements punctuating the pervasive stillness as most of the city slumbered. Parked outside the Eight Dragons restaurant, Jax's car was the lone vehicle on the street. The restaurant, ostensibly closed for renovations as indicated by a sign out front, showed signs of life through a flickering light visible from the front window.

Inside, Yan provided the only illumination, holding up a burning candle. She and Jax paused just inside the entrance, surveying the chaos—broken items littered the floor, and their elongated, spooky shadows danced on the walls under the candlelight.

"I can't believe how scary this is," Jax whispered.

Unfazed, Doc moved ahead, setting down a bag he was carrying. He rummaged in his flak jacket for a cigarette lighter, then extracted sticks of incense from the bag, lighting them.

"Place them in a four-metre diameter circle on the floor, Doc," Yan instructed. "Jax, position the fruit inside the circle."

Doc muttered under his breath as he complied. "I can't believe I'm doing this ... All to attract an evil spirit ... and I don't even believe in ghosts."

Yan came up behind Doc. "Are you done?"

Doc jumped. "Ah! Don't do that!"

"Glad nothing scares you. Makes me feel super secure," Jax said sarcastically, arranging fruit from the bag.

"Put a sock in it, Jax," Doc retorted. "Alright, Yan, they're set up. Now what do we do?"

"We sit and wait," Yan replied calmly.

She guided them through the dimly lit space to the nearest table, setting the candle down before they each took a seat.

"We could try a séance," Jax joked half-heartedly.

Yan looked at them seriously, the candlelight casting eerie shadows on her face. "When the ghost appears, I will see it. I will watch it take the food ... then, I will burn money as an offering to it. This will make it happy and keep it here," she explained, pulling a 30 cm x 30 cm mirror from the bag Doc had carried in. "Then you must each do your part quickly. Jax, you will hold the mirror. Doc, you will light the fireworks and throw them into the ring of incense. When the fireworks go off, the spirit will be so frightened it will fly towards the mirror, thinking it is the way out. A spirit cannot see its own reflection. Once the ghost is in the mirror, Jax, you must smash it on the floor... and the ghost will be trapped there in the pieces forever. Okay?"

"No. I feel like an idiot," Doc complained.

"That's okay, Doc," Jax said. "You should be used to that by now."

"Ha, ha," Doc retorted cynically, their banter amusing Yan.

Suddenly, Yan's expression changed to one of alertness. "Shush! I can feel something. Do you feel it? The cold."

Jax looked at her forearm in the candlelight, noticing her hairs standing on end and goosebumps. She showed Doc. "Yep, you bet I can feel it," she said nervously.

"The ghost is here," Yan whispered, her eyes darting towards the entrance.

A blurry apparition, visible only to Yan, began to emerge from the floor. Struggling through the solid surface, it finally broke free and glided towards the last remaining fish tank. With a sudden, forceful impact, the tank shattered, spilling water and sending lobsters scrambling across the floor. Then, with a series of loud bangs, three fluorescent ceiling light tubes overhead burst, showering Yan, Jax, and Doc with shards of glass. They instinctively covered their faces to shield their eyes from the debris. Jax cautiously peeked through her fingers, while Doc remained seated, his arms folded across his chest, his expression one of scepticism.

"This is bullshit," he muttered.

"Quiet, Doc ... It has seen the food ... It's calming down," Yan instructed.

The ghost glided towards Jax. Yan recognised him as a Chinaman, adorned in traditional Chinese garb from the 19th century.

"He's right beside you, Jax. Concentrate, and you will see him."

Still peering through her trembling fingers, Jax screeched, "No, no, I can't ... I'm too frightened."

As the ghost passed through Jax, she shivered. "What was that?" she shrieked.

Whoosh! The candle extinguished.

Jax's hair stood on end. "Ah! What's it doing!"

"Relax, relax, it's only static electricity," Doc assured, pragmatically.

Yan observed the ghost's every movement. "Get ready! He's going for the food."

The ethereal ghost floated towards the ring of incense, paused, and hovered. Despite its opacity, Yan could discern its face: piercing eyes, a sinister expression, long hair splaying wildly, and a mouth of decayed teeth. Its malevolent grin intensified at the sight of the food, though it seemed cautious of the incense. Yan waited patiently for it to glide into the ring, then swiftly produced a handful of lucky money from her pocket, igniting it with a lighter. "Come on, guys!"

Doc prepared the fireworks, and Jax, summoning her courage, grasped the mirror. They joined Yan. But as they approached, Yan screamed and was hurled backward onto the ground, as if shoved by an invisible force. Tables scattered, creating a path for the ghost's escape. Items crashed, then, the room fell silent.

Doc cradled Yan in his arms.

Jax, hand on her chest and heart pounding, shrieked, "What just happened? I'm freaking out here!"

Yan lay unconscious. Doc attempted to rouse her. "Yan ... Yan ... are you okay?"

"Why not try some CPR?" Jax suggested, her tone laced with cynicism.

"Good idea," Doc agreed, then leaned over Yan, appearing to kiss rather than administer CPR. He glanced up at Jax. "Hmm, tasty, she had garlic with her dinner."

"Yeah right ... come on, what are you doing, sticking around for dessert?"

Doc noticed a cord on the floor sparking. "Check that," he directed, pointing at Yan's previous location. "A live wire. She must have stepped on it and received an electric shock."

Yan's eyes flickered open, and she sat up, feeling the back of her head. "Ew, what's this unpleasant taste in my mouth?"

Jax smirked at Doc. "Garlic, huh?"

"It attacked me, I fell and hit my head. Are you guys okay?"

"Take it easy, Yan ... you've had a shock," Doc advised.

"No, no, I'm fine. Ghosts don't shock me at all; I've seen stacks of them."

Doc, shaking his head, assisted her to stand. "No, it's likely you stepped on that live wire there ... Everything is shorting out ... the fluorescent lights, the aerator in the tank. That's what caused the explosion ... This place is a serious fire hazard. We should leave."

"I'm with you," Jax agreed.

"No way, we need to find its lair. Trust me. This is a malevolent spirit. If we don't exorcise it, it's going to kill someone."

The girls exchanged a look of dread, while Doc maintained the expression of a total sceptic.

CHAPTER
SIX

The next day, Jax, Yan, and Doc stood before the security door of Wang Jewels, located on the third floor of the Regency Building in Chinatown. Doc offered a genial wave to the security camera above the door, and a resonant 'click' signalled their admittance. Their purpose was to meet Mr Wang, a representative of the Chinatown Business Association, which had enlisted Xiang and Yan's services to dispel the Eight Dragons' troublesome ghost.

Inside the opulently adorned boutique, Mr Wang welcomed them. "Good morning, please follow me," he said.

They trailed him into a sumptuously appointed boardroom, where jasmine tea awaited them.

"After receiving your call this morning, I secured a copy of the blueprint you requested from the water board. Understandably, you wanted a map of the sewage system beneath Chinatown, suspecting it houses the ghost," Mr Wang articulated.

"That's correct, Mr Wang. Yan suspects the ghost's lair might be near or under the Eight Dragons," Jax interjected.

"And your perspective, Mr Lee? As a scientist?" Mr Wang queried.

"My candid view, Mr Wang, is there's no malevolent spirit. A more mundane explanation is the antiquated electrical system in the restaurant," Doc replied.

"How would you react if I revealed that in 1849, a fugitive Chinese criminal was abandoned to perish in the Tank Stream tunnel beneath Sydney?" Mr Wang posed.

Yan unrolled the sewage plan across the boardroom table.

"The Tank Stream was Sydney's sole freshwater source at that time, right?" Jax inquired.

"So, you're implying this is a vengeful haunting by that outlaw? Absurd," Doc remarked, sceptical.

Mr Wang handed Doc a timeworn book, opened to a specific page. "This is the 'Australian Dictionary of Dates from 1542 to May 1879', first published in 1879."

Doc scrutinised the book for authenticity.

"Yes, it's genuine, indeed."

"But why would it begin in 1542 when the British started their occupation in 1770?" Jax pondered.

Doc found the relevant passage and read aloud, "Here's the reference that explains it under 'Australia, First Maps of.' 'The earliest map of Australia, now in the British Museum and bearing the arms of the Dauphin of France, appears to have been created during the reign of Francis I for his son, the Dauphin. Its probable date is 1530. A map of Australia dedicated to Henry VIII of England, evidently a copy of the Dauphin map, was executed by a Frenchman named Jean Rotz, who came to England. This map bears the date 1542. On this significant map, the large landmass was called 'Java de Grande,' distinct from a smaller island named 'Lytll Java.'"

Jax crossed her arms defensively. "Yeah, they forgot to notice there were already other people living here."

"Please proceed to the page I have marked, Doctor Lee," Mr Wang requested.

"Under the heading of Crimes and Criminals, Remarkable ... 'Three native women and a police officer were murdered by Chinese, Tsin Fu Chin in 1849. Chin was apprehended and cuffed near to the gallows, corner of Park and Castlereagh streets but escaped into the Tank Stream tunnel nearby where he is thought to have perished.' That doesn't prove anything," Doc dismissed.

"Except that it is a probable explanation from our point of view as to why we have been harassed by this obviously deranged spirit for over 150 years," Wang proposed.

"Yes, the account makes perfect sense. The ghost is angry, but I think because he died such a miserable death while being handcuffed ... I expect he might have been eaten alive by rats," Yan added.

"Ew! How gross. What a way to go!" Jax exclaimed.

Wang pointed at the map. "If you look here, the Tank Stream runs directly under where Chinatown is today ... and if you look even closer, you can see a tunnel goes directly under the Eight Dragons Restaurant."

They all scrutinised the plan.

"Look here," Jax said. "If you follow the tunnel from just near the corner of Park and Castlereagh streets, it's a direct line to Chinatown ... He would definitely have run that way. Was Chinatown here in 1849?"

"I believe there was a small Chinese settlement with businesses, so yes," Wang confirmed.

"That might explain why he ran that way. He probably hoped to hide amongst his fellow countrymen," Yan theorised.

Jax gazed into Yan's eyes with a new understanding. "Maybe they didn't help him?"

"Yes, yes, that would certainly explain why he has continued to haunt them, they might have left him to die down there," Yan concurred.

"I think we have too many presumptions and far too little evidence," Doc remarked.

Yan thought about it for a moment, then her eyes locked with Jax's. "We have to go into the tunnel."

Jax stared back, wide-eyed. "The sewer ... full of rats and a total gross-out? No way."

Yan nodded firmly.

Doc, still examining the plan, pointed out, "There's an entrance to the tunnel right here."

CHAPTER
SEVEN

As Jax, Yan, and Doc exited the Regency Building onto the bustling Goulburn Street, Yan paused. "Let's get a coffee and make a plan."

"I have a meeting this morning, and besides, I won't be able to come tonight," Doc declared.

Jax was taken aback. "Why not?"

"Because I don't agree with it, Jax," Doc elaborated, his tone laced with scepticism. "Look, the ghost theory just doesn't add up. To me, the most plausible explanation for the incident we experienced is faulty electrical wiring."

"Didn't you feel a presence?" Jax countered, her frustration palpable.

Yan, accustomed to dealing with sceptics, especially those with a scientific mindset like Doc, gently grasped Jax's arm. "It's okay. Doc has a perspective different from ours, and that's fine. I wish we could persuade you to join us tonight. If you change your mind, we'll meet right here at 2 a.m."

Doc extended his hand to Jax. "Thanks, Jax, it's been interesting. Nice to meet you, Yan. I hope Xiang is okay."

They watched him walk away. Yan, still holding Jax's arm, offered a reassuring smile. "All good, now let's find a café."

Nestled in the Daily Grind Café with coffees in hand, Jax confided to Yan, "I'd feel more at ease with Doc with us tonight."

Yan, ever the optimist, reassured her, "We'll manage. I've dealt with similar situations before. Two years ago in San Francisco, I accompanied Pop into the sewers."

"Were you chasing a ghost?" Jax inquired, her interest piqued.

"No, it was a demon. It was inadvertently summoned during a séance and fled into the sewer system," Yan clarified.

Jax was visibly shocked. "Really? And you actually went down there? Did you catch it?"

"We did. We trapped it in a tunnel. Pop used an incantation to vanquish it," Yan recounted.

"What became of the demon?"

"It disintegrated into a cloud of dust," Yan described, her hands illustrating the explosion. Jax listened intently, captivated by every detail. Their conversation was suddenly interrupted by Yan's phone ringing. After a short conversation, Yan looked up at Jax, "That was the hospital. They're releasing Pop. I need to go pick him up."

Standing, she continued, "I'll see you outside the Regency Building at midnight. We might need some items for tonight. I'll consult Pop and send you a list, okay?"

"Wait, you've done this before, right?" Jax questioned, her voice tinged with concern.

Yan hesitated, "Well, not exactly ... I've been with Pop when he did. Don't worry, Jax. See you later," she said with a hint of levity, leaving Jax somewhat unsettled, particularly with Doc having jumped ship.

In her compact office at NewsLine, Jax sat behind her small desk, her eyes fixed on her laptop screen. The tidier surroundings mirrored her recent efforts to instil some semblance of order in her professional life. For the past hour, she had been immersed in researching exorcisms, but the more she delved into the topic, the more bewildered she became.

Her search was inundated with details about Catholic exorcisms, along with a plethora of YouTube videos. These included harrowing scenes from films such as "The Exorcist," which did little to calm her nerves. Watching the infamous scene where Linda Blair's head turned a full 360 degrees only intensified Jax's apprehension about the impending supernatural venture.

Her unease grew as she read about the nine deaths linked to the production of "The Exorcist," encompassing a technician, a nightwatchman, and several cast members. These eerie coincidences added a chilling layer to her already heightened anxiety.

Jax had consulted Ai Grok about the repercussions of trying to vanquish a ghost. The response she received highlighted that vanquishing a ghost could have repercussions depending on cultural beliefs and personal views. While there was no scientific evidence supporting the existence of ghosts, the cultural context could lead to various consequences. This made Jax think of Doc and whether his scepticism might be justified. As she mulled over these thoughts, Tilly entered the room with a cheerful "Knock, knock!" and commented on the tidiness of the office. Tilly sat down, eager for an update on Jax's first mission.

As Jax recounted her encounter with the ghost and Yan's plan, Tilly's reaction was unexpected. She sat motionless, her face as if she had seen a ghost herself. When Jax asked if she believed in ghosts, she nodded and genuflected, revealing a deep-seated belief in the supernatural.

Jax, curious, asked Ai Grok about Filipinos and ghosts. The AI explained that Filipinos, with their rich cultural heritage influenced by indigenous, Catholic, and Chinese traditions, do believe in ghosts. This includes beliefs in various supernatural beings and practices during festivals like the Chinese Hungry Ghost Festival. Jax was intrigued by the similarities between Filipino and Chinese beliefs in ghosts.

Tilly shared a Filipino superstition against leaving doors open at night to prevent ghosts or evil spirits from entering. When Jax mentioned that Doc wouldn't be joining them because he didn't believe in ghosts, Tilly revealed that Doc was half Filipino, half Chinese, and likely did believe in ghosts but was just scared.

This revelation left Jax pondering if Tilly might be right about Doc's reasons for bailing out.

Doc had just finished an interview with HR at The Genesis Institute, where he hoped to gain employment as a junior researcher while completing his degree at the university. As he was leaving the office, his phone rang.

"Hello?"

"Doctor Lee, this is Mr Chow, we met yesterday at the hospital. Mr Wang and I are representatives of the Chinatown business Association."

"Yes, Mr Chow, I remember. But before you say anything, I should inform you I'm off that case."

"Really?"

"Yes, I was only onboard to provide my scientific opinion, which is no longer required."

"That is the precise reason for my call. Can we meet for an urgent private discussion?"

Doc glanced at his watch; it was 2:30 pm. "I suppose so, but it will need to be brief."

"That's no problem. How about 5 pm at your favourite pub?"

"The Friend in Hand, fine. At the main bar," Doc agreed, wondering to himself how Mr Chow knew The Friend in Hand was his watering hole.

CHAPTER EIGHT

Yan helped Xiang out of a taxi and into the Observatory Hotel. Once settled in their suite, Xiang took a seat in a lounge chair while Yan updated him on the Eight Dragons ghost case. Xiang felt apprehensive, not confident that Yan and Jax could stand up to the ghost, especially after what it had done to him. He knew it would be a formidable challenge.

Yan, on the other hand, was confident in her training under Xiang.

"The problem with confronting the ghost in its lair is you will only have one chance to defeat it. If you fail, the ghost will be alerted to its exposure … they do not like being recognised because that can lead to identifying them. Knowing who a ghost was in its human form provides the means of eliminating it."

"I understand, Pop. You taught me well; I know what to do."

"That I believe, Yan, you can see the ghost … you have the gift … but I worry for yours and Jax's safety."

"We have no choice, Pop. Please, we should make a list of what I will need tonight."

When Doc stepped off his bike in the car park of the Friend in Hand Pub, he was unexpectedly ambushed by two burly men. They quickly manhandled him into the back of a black SUV.

Sitting opposite him inside was a man in a dark suit who had gangster written all over him.

"What's this all about?" Doc asked, trying to remain calm.

"Doctor Lee, though you're not really a doctor yet, are you? In fact, you've only recently graduated from high school," the man in the suit remarked, scrutinizing him as if he were an object up for sale at an auction.

"So, what business is that of yours? You know who I am; you have the advantage. Who are you?"

"Questions, Doc, questions. Your inquisitive mind brims with them. Do you realise they could be perilous, potentially fatal even?" the man retorted, his voice dripping with icy undertones.

Doc folded his arms defensively. "Listen, whoever you are, this gangster stuff is reserved for Netflix. This is Sydney, it won't..."

Before he could finish, the man's expression hardened. He reached into his inside coat pocket, drew a revolver, and aimed it at Doc. "Maybe this will convince you otherwise. You were here to meet Mr Chow. Well, I have Mr Chow, and if you don't do what I ask of you, Mr Chow will become the new ghost of the Eight Dragons. Do you understand me, Mr Lee?"

Realising the gravity of the situation, Doc acknowledged that the man meant business. "What is it you want from me?"

"We want the ghost to continue with its haunting," the man stated plainly.

Doc frowned, confused. "I don't get it. Why?"

"Do you know Mr Lao?"

"No, who is Mr Lao?"

"The owner of the Eight Dragons restaurant."

"Never met him."

"Well, Mr Lao doesn't rent the restaurant; he owns the freehold. He inherited it from his father, who inherited it from his father, and so on ... a generational owner."

"So?"

"I'll leave it for you to work out. You have until tomorrow to ensure Xiang Zi and his daughter leave Australia; otherwise, it will be at the peril of Mr Chow, and he won't be the last. Goodbye, Mr Lee."

As the car door swung open and Doc was set free, he found himself standing alone in the car park, contemplating the severity of the threat and the enigmatic circumstances enveloping the Eight Dragons and its spectral presence.

Jax was in a convenience store in Chinatown, gathering the final items on Yan's list, when her phone rang. It was Yan, bearing unsettling news: Mr. Lao, proprietor of the Eight Dragons restaurant, had revealed that Mr Chow had been abducted. Perplexed, Jax queried, "Why? For what reason?"

"The abductors are demanding that we leave on the earliest flight, no later than tomorrow morning. They also demanded that we do not exorcise the ghost," Yan explained.

"I don't get it," Jax admitted, her confusion evident.

"I don't either, but he didn't say much more than that. I'm making the arrangements to now leave. The first flight to San Francisco is at 11 am tomorrow."

Jax felt a mix of relief and anger. She was relieved to avoid the daunting sewer expedition, yet incensed by the kidnappers' demands. "Oh well, I just bought the last item on your list."

"Good; we'll still need them," Yan asserted resolutely.

"What for?" Jax inquired, taken aback.

"We've got a ghost to vanquish."

Meanwhile, Mr Wang had also received an intimidating phone call from the kidnapper, which left him feeling anxious and alarmed. The kidnapper had ominously cautioned that failure to comply with his demands would result in harm not only to Mr Chow but also potentially to Wang's family. Wang promptly contacted Xiang to apprise him of the dire situation.

Xiang, seasoned in handling such perilous circumstances, counselled Wang to remain with his family and to avoid involving the police. He assured him that he and Yan would depart for San Francisco at 11 am the following day, confident that this action would defuse the situation.

Throughout the call, Xiang's calm demeanour was apparent, indicating that this was not his first encounter with such hazardous predicaments. His experience and poise hinted at a history of managing high-stakes situations, revealing a readiness to take whatever steps necessary to guarantee everyone's well-being.

CHAPTER
NINE

The city streets were deserted at that early hour, casting an eerie curtain of silence over Jax and Yan. Jax, dressed like a hiker with a backpack, closed the boot of her car.

"Got everything?" Yan asked.

"Yes, I checked it off your list as I packed it all," Jax confirmed.

They began walking towards the Regency Building, the entrance to the sewer. As they rounded a corner, Jax suddenly stopped Yan, her voice tinged with worry. "There's someone standing out front of the building."

Yan squinted at the silhouetted figure. "It might be someone sent to stop us from entering the sewer."

"What will we do?" Jax asked, nervously.

"Wait here, I'll find out," Yan said with a hint of bravery.

"Don't be ridiculous, he might be a gangster," Jax protested.

"It's okay, Jax," Yan reassured her. "I have a black belt in martial arts. I can handle myself. Wait here." With that, Yan headed towards the dark figure.

Jax waited anxiously, biting her knuckle and ready to flee if things turned south. To her surprise, she saw Yan waving her over. After a quick glance behind for any lurking danger, she hurried to join Yan.

Upon reaching them, Jax realised Yan was talking to Doc and instantly relaxed.

"Changed your mind, huh?" Jax remarked, interrupting Doc's explanation.

"I was just telling Yan, I was forced into the back of a car by a pair of thugs. There was a guy in a suit who pulled a gun on me. He told me to leave the ghost alone," Doc shared.

"This must be the same guy that threatened Pop," Yan deduced.

"And kidnapped Mr Chow, and then threatened Mr Lao, the owner of the Eight Dragons," Jax added.

"I don't get it, why? Who is this guy?" Yan wondered aloud.

"I think I get it," Doc mused. "I think this gangster wants to buy the Eight Dragons and wants the price to drop. No-one would want to buy it with its haunted reputation."

"That makes sense. Who would buy a haunted restaurant?" Jax agreed.

"Well, haunted maybe, but even if it isn't, the rumour has been enough to close it down," Doc speculated.

"Right, so they wouldn't want the ghost exorcised," Yan concluded.

"It's probably them creating the mayhem to perpetuate the myth," Doc maintained, still sceptical of the ghost's existence.

"Jax, give me the key," Yan requested.

Jax unzipped her backpack and handed over a metal key.

"What's that for?" Doc inquired.

"We got it from the waterboard to open the manhole to the sewer."

"You're not seriously considering going through with this, are you?" Doc asked, his voice laden with incredulity.

Yan took the key, knelt down to the circular manhole in the pavement, and inserted it into the keyhole. "Sure am."

"You're mental," Doc muttered.

"Help me lift this," Yan asked.

Together, the trio laboured to pry the manhole cover open. Jax retrieved a torch from her backpack and shone its beam down the hole, unveiling metal rungs descending into the gloom. "It seems like a long way down... and dark," she uttered apprehensively, her voice echoing in the void.

Yan stood up. "Look, I'm not here to convince you there is a ghost, Doc, but we could sure use your help. There are lives at stake here, whether you believe it or not. One way or another, we need to find out, and this is the best way to do it."

Doc, seeing the reason in her words, relented. "Okay, okay, I'll come. Let's get on with it."

"Good. Now listen up, we are only going to get one shot at this, so we have make it work. If we fail, the ghost will move elsewhere in the tunnel system, and we might never find it again." Jax handed Yan and Doc a torch each. They switched them on, and with Yan leading, they climbed in one at a time. Doc went last to close the manhole cover, leaving Goulburn Street deathly quiet.

Once at the base of the ladder, they found themselves in a narrow tunnel. They checked the map Yan had copied from the larger one Wang had given her. Once the route was agreed upon, Doc took the lead.

Their footsteps echoed in the dark tunnel, underscored by the sound of running water. Doc pointed the flashlight ahead, revealing the path before them.

"We should come to the Tank Stream at a junction up ahead. From there, we take the left fork, right?" Doc asked.

Yan checked the map and confirmed, "Yes."

Jax flashed her torch at a noise, illuminating thousands of fleeing cockroaches. "Ew ... I hate cockroaches. Phew, the smell in here is seriously gross."

"You'll get used to it," Doc said.

Yan chuckled, "All men say that."

As they reached the intersection of three tunnels, the Tank Stream widened into a larger tunnel that forked to the left. Doc, leading the way, shined his torch down the left branch before stepping into it.

A short distance along the narrow path beside which flowed the Tank Stream, Doc shined his torch up, revealing a manhole in the ceiling. "Right. Three more of these manholes will put us directly under the Eight Dragons," he calculated.

As they passed by a sewer pipe discharging into the stream, Jax heard a disturbing sound. She quickly turned her torch towards the noise, revealing hundreds of red eyes and the sound of scratching emanating from inside the pipe. "Look at this," she called out.

Doc hurried back to her side took a quick look and immediately recognised the impending threat. "Rats! Hundreds of them ... coming our way. They're probably attracted by our scent," he presumed.

"Speak for yourself," Jax retorted half-jokingly, her nerves on edge. "Get moving!"

They hustled along the tunnel, Doc glancing at the ceiling for more markers while Jax periodically checked behind them with her torch. Suddenly, she stopped. "Oh, crap," she grumbled.

Yan and Doc stopped and looked back. Jax's torch showed rats pouring out of the sewer pipe, swarming towards them. "They look hungry," Yan observed calmly.

"Come on, get going!" Doc barked urgently.

They sprinted along the tunnel until they reached another intersection. Doc, panting, shined his torch at a manhole in the ceiling. "This is it ... the third manhole ... That small tunnel to the right leads directly under the restaurant."

Yan inspected the narrow tunnel with her torch, revealing a floor littered with decaying fruit and other offerings. Pointing the torch upward, she spotted a pipe extending from above. "This is where they've been giving offerings to the ghost. That pipe must come from the restaurant ... look." She illuminated the ground. "Years and years of food offerings."

"Yeah, they've been feeding the rats and cockroaches," Doc commented.

Yan suddenly looked up in fright. The ghost flew at speed from out of the dark tunnel, picked her up bodily, and bashed her hard against the wall. It then flew back inside the narrow dark tunnel as Yan slid down the wall onto the slimy floor, unconscious.

Doc rushed to her, lifting her head gently. He withdrew his hand, now stained with blood.

Jax asked worriedly, "What happened?"

"I don't know, she just jumped backwards like something gave her a fright and hit her head on that pipe there. It doesn't look good."

"Was it the ghost?" Jax asked, fearfully.

The sound of squeaking and scurrying rats was growing louder. Doc shook his head in confusion. "I don't know, I don't know…"

Jax shined her torch behind them, there were hordes of rats closing in on them. She screeched, "The rats!"

Yan stirred.

"Yan ... speak..." Doc said, trying to sit her up.

"Jax, you must do the job for me," Yan mumbled groggily. "Go into the tunnel under the restaurant. You know what to do ... I'm, I'm feeling too faint—" Her voice trailed off as she passed out.

"Help me lift her, she's got concussion, we'll go back ... it's no use," Doc decided.

The clamour of the approaching rats intensified. Jax, her resolve strengthening, rummaged through the backpack, pulled out a string of fireworks, and handed it to Doc. "Feed this to the rats. I'm going after that ghost."

"Why?"

"Because that's what we came here to do!" she declared, heading determinedly into the dark, narrow tunnel.

CHAPTER
TEN

Doc spun around to confront the rats, with hundreds of red eyes converging on him. He ignited the belt of fireworks and hurled it at them.

Meanwhile, Jax, brushing cobwebs aside in the extremely narrow tunnel that barely accommodated her, flinched as the loud rat-a-tat-tat of the fireworks echoed through the tunnels. She quickly realised it was Doc's handiwork.

Muttering to herself in an effort to remain calm and determined, Jax whispered, "Right, it's just the fireworks ... Keep moving, Jax." The ground was sludgy, the stench revolting, making it difficult for her to breathe. The thought of where the spiders that spun the large webs might be lingered in her mind. Spiders were another of her pet hates. Her torchlight revealed an ancient chalk drawing of a dragon on the wall, prompting her to halt. "Wow, that looks really old." Beside the dragon, Chinese script and the date 1892 were visible. She shined her torch on the ground, uncovering a pile of decayed rags and bones. "Far out. Hello, Mr Fung Chin." Gently, she nudged the rags with her foot, revealing a rusted pair of handcuffs. She picked them up, placing them in her backpack, then withdrew sticks of incense, and began arranging them in a small circle.

Meanwhile, Doc, bearing Yan in his arms into the main tunnel, carefully laid her down and aimed his torch at an approaching second wave of rats. Igniting another string of fireworks, he exclaimed, "Take this!" and tossed it towards them. The rapid rat-a-tat-rat-a-tat resonated like machine gun fire in the confined space, and the resulting blaze, casting vivid flashes on the tunnel walls, sent the rats scurrying frantically back into the sewer pipe.

In the narrow tunnel, Jax sat on the ground, legs crossed, surrounded by the smouldering incense and fresh food offerings. She flinched at the sound of exploding fireworks, amplified by the tunnel's acoustics. Closing her eyes, she tried to refocus on her meditation.

Suddenly, the dragon petroglyph on the wall shimmered, and a plasma-like energy formed, materialising into a floating, rotating ball. From this ethereal orb, the size of a soccer ball, the ghost of a Chinese man in 19th-century attire emerged, floating and seemingly disoriented. It then noticed the food inside the ring.

Jax gradually opened her eyes and, to her amazement and horror, beheld the ghost. "Oh my God," she uttered aloud in disbelief. "I can actually see it. Xiang was right." This was a profound moment of realisation for her, exactly as Xiang had foretold. Through meditation, she truly possessed the ability to perceive spirits.

The ghost drifted into the circle and started to consume the fruit. Jax, with cautious and measured movements to avoid alarming the spirit, retrieved some 'happy money' from her pocket, lit it, and waved it around to capture the ghost's attention. The ghost glanced at her sharply, apparently under the impression it was unseen by Jax. It opened its mouth, revealing decayed teeth, and emitted a silent laugh. In a moment of daring, Jax swiftly lit a string of fireworks, hurling them into the circle with a sense of urgency. She then grabbed a mirror, brandishing it like a shield. With a defiant cry, "Come on, Mr Chin!" she challenged the ghost. The spectral figure, evidently recognizing its name, fixed her with a chilling, sinister stare.

As the fireworks erupted in a cacophony of sound and light, the ghost recoiled in terror. Its ethereal form twisted and writhed, then, in a frenzied panic, it hurtled straight towards the mirror. With an eerie silence, it vanished into the glassy surface.

Jax, her heart pounding, didn't hesitate. She threw the mirror with all her might against the ancient dragon image on the wall. The glass shattered into a thousand sparkling shards, each piece reflecting the fleeting image of the trapped ghost.

Breathless and drained, Jax collapsed against the cold wall. Her mind was a whirlwind of fatigue and relief, so intense that even the sight of cockroaches skittering across the damp floor couldn't rouse her usual revulsion.

Jax, Doc, Yan, Xiang, Mr Wang, and Mr Chow sat around a table, savouring a lavish Peking Duck feast at the Golden Dragon Restaurant. Mr Lao entered the private room to join them.

"So, the Golden Dragon Restaurant is also under your ownership, Mr Lao?" Xiang inquired.

"Yes, I am fortunate to own two establishments. I am deeply grateful for your role in preserving the Eight Dragons," Mr Lao responded.

Xiang looked towards Doc. "It wasn't solely my doing, Mr Lao. These three young individuals played a pivotal role. By the way, Doc, are you still harbouring any scepticism?"

Doc offered a smile towards Jax, then to Yan. "Absolutely."

"Perhaps you think we concocted the ghost story to refurbish the restaurant under the guise of an insurance claim?" Mr Lao joked with Doc.

"Hadn't considered that, but it's possible. Regardless, everything resolved well. Xiang's health improved ... Yan may have a headache but agreed to a date with me ... Jax secured her debut story for NewsLine ... and Mr Chow was safely released."

Mr Chow nodded in agreement, "And the ghost has departed."

Wang added, "It was fortunate you were aware of the prospective buyer for the Eight Dragons, Mr Lao. It aided the police in liberating Mr Chow."

Lao shook his head, "I had only one interested party as I wasn't actively selling. The abduction of Mr Chow was a misguided strategy."

"Who was behind the kidnapping?" Jax queried.

"Diàn Xiàn Shī," Lao revealed. "Diàn signifies 'to disrupt', Xiàn represents 'line' or 'thread', indicating his criminal network's complexity, and Shī means 'master', highlighting his influential role."

"The name sounds more imposing than his deeds," Xiang quipped.

"He operates several mah-jong schools, the primary one being Fortune Court. I suspect his aim was to acquire a thriving restaurant to legitimise his operations."

"I believe he is looking for a front to launder illicit funds," Wang interjected.

Xiang stood up, raising his glass. "A toast to my new apprentice, Jax, who opened her mind to discern the truth."

They all raised their glasses in tribute.

"So, Jax, do you truly believe we encountered the ghost of Tsin Fu Chin?" Lao questioned.

Jax retrieved a cardboard box from her bag and handed it to Lao. He opened it and announced, "The fragments of the mirror!"

"The spirit remains trapped within," Xiang clarified. "It's imperative, Mr Lao, that you safeguard these pieces. Should they be reassembled, the ghost would be unleashed, and it would be as mad as hell."

A round of chuckles followed.

"Ha. You guys are spinning an urban legend. I doubt Mr Chin ever set foot in that tunnel," Doc remarked, somewhat dismissively.

Jax held up the set of rusted handcuffs to him.

"Oh, I'm not so sure about that, Mr Sceptic. These handcuffs date back to the 1840s ... That's some proof."

"Hmm, maybe I was wrong. As Confucius says, 'There's a first time for everything.'"

Their laughter filled the room.

"Xiang, do I still have spirits clinging to my back?" Jax asked, turning sideways for his inspection.

"Doc has plenty, but you Jax are the moon," Xiang responded enigmatically.

Doc playfully shook himself like a dog, prompting more laughter. "That should do it ... Now, I can finally get back to some serious work."

Jax passed him a newspaper clipping. "Not so fast, buddy ... Take a look at this."

He read it out loud, "The Boulia Times: 'Wife claims Scientist husband abducted by Aliens'. Right, aliens in Boulia? Where on Earth is Boulia?"

"Western Queensland. I've booked us a flight there tomorrow morning. I'll pick you up at 7 am?" Jax said with a cheeky grin.

"Over my dead body ... You're more likely to find Elvis than get me on another one of your wild adventures."

MIN MIN

CHAPTER
ONE

Daniel teased his new wife with a playful shout, "Come on! Pedal faster, keep up…" He was a good distance ahead on the long road slicing through the desert, bathed in the fading glow of sunset.

"How far to the town? My legs are aching," Justine called back, her voice echoing with a mix of fatigue and worry. "I really don't want to be out here when it gets dark."

Daniel paused his bike on the crest of a small hill, turning to look back at Justine, who was laboriously pedalling up towards him. Suddenly, she stopped, shielding her eyes from glare, and cried out in alarm, "Behind you!"

Daniel whipped his head around, heart racing. Approaching him were two mesmerising lights, silent and enigmatic, moving along the road in an area infamous for the Min Min lights. He watched, transfixed, as the lights advanced with an eerie grace.

From her position at the base of the hill, Justine saw Daniel's silhouette bathed in a large, luminous glow.

The stillness was abruptly shattered by a deafening roar. A colossal cattle truck with blazing headlights burst over the hill, its diesel engine thundering. The truck enveloped Daniel and Justine in a whirlwind of red dust, leaving them coughing and spluttering in its wake. Amidst the settling dust, Daniel, chuckling despite the shock, called out, "You all right, love?"

Gasping for air, Justine replied, her voice laced with disbelief, "We could've been flattened! That thing was a monster."

Darkness descended rapidly, the sun vanishing behind the horizon in mere minutes. Daniel surveyed the road ahead. "I can see Boulia's lights, all three of them," he joked, trying to lighten the mood. "Come on, let's keep moving."

He was about to pedal off when a sudden, inexplicable feeling halted him. A faint, continuous drone filled the air, reminiscent of a didgeridoo. A warm breeze, unusual for the evening, carried the sound towards them. Justine's anxious voice interrupted his contemplation.

"Daniel? Daniel … what's that?" she asked, pointing to their left.

Daniel turned and saw, to his amazement, two perfectly spherical orbs of light floating about six metres above the ground, not more than twenty metres away.

"They must be the Min Min lights!" he exclaimed, a mix of awe and excitement in his voice. As he watched, the lights began to drift further towards Boulia. Seized by curiosity, Daniel hopped back on his bike and followed.

Justine, reaching the top of the hill, expected to see Daniel ahead. Instead, she found his bike deserted on the roadside. "Daniel? Daniel!" she screamed, her voice trembling with fear. Then she noticed the lights, now numbering three, hovering silently to her left.

"Daniel!" she screamed again, her plea echoing into the night. "Please, bring him back! Don't take him!"

Lugging their small bags, Jax and Doc stepped off the chartered Beechcraft Baron G58 and wheeling their bags behind them, headed towards what served as a terminal here—a simple tin shed. The oppressive heat hit them like a ton of bricks, accompanied by a relentless swarm of annoying flies buzzing around their faces.

"They say folks here are so out of the way, they applaud when they spot a stranger," Jax joked, trying to lighten the mood.

"I can't believe you got me into this. How are we even going to get into town?" Doc muttered, swiping at the flies in annoyance.

"Chill, mate. It's not the end of the world. I've ordered a taxi," Jax said, trying to calm him.

They found a bench under the tin shed's shade and sat down to wait. Off in the distance, the Beechcraft zoomed down the runway, its image shimmering in the heat rising off the tarmac.

As the sound of the plane's engines faded, the persistent drone of flies seemed to intensify.

"You do get that we're going to die here, today, like right now? It's boiling, and I'm dehydrating by the second … I'll be dust in minutes. I'd feel lighter if it weren't for the ton of flies on my back," Doc grumbled, his mood sour.

Jax thought he was funny and chuckled. "Oh, stop moaning. Look, there's a car coming."

Doc peered out at the vast, flat horizon blending into the clear blue sky but couldn't see anything. "Where?"

Jax stood, grabbing her bag. "It's almost here. You ready?"

"Hold up. Your flies are all flocking to me now," Doc complained, just as he noticed a car appearing in the distance. "How'd you spot that?"

"Just had a feeling. It's a Koorie thing."

Bouncing along the dirt track, they breathed a sigh of relief when they finally hit bitumen. The transition to the smoother road made conversation easier without the risk of biting their tongues.

Doc, seated in the front passenger seat of the white 2009 VE Commodore station wagon, scrutinised the driver. Decked out in an aged, moth-eaten army slouch hat, a grubby, off-white singlet, khaki shorts, and work boots, the driver's forearms were as beefy as a body-builder's. He nonchalantly chewed on a toothpick.

"You plan to be in town long?" the driver asked in a distinctive country drawl.

Jax, from the back seat, answered, "Only a few days. Did you hear about the abduction ... um?"

"Bluey Wilson. The only taxi in town. Yep, heard about it. Drove him around for a bit," the driver affirmed.

Doc, peering out at the flat expanse, asked, "What's your take on what really happened, Bluey?"

After a pause, Bluey replied, "Not sure. Best you talk to Sergeant Wilson at the police station."

"Fair enough," Doc conceded. "How much further to town?"

"Just beyond the jump-up over there," Bluey mumbled around the toothpick.

Doc guessed he meant the few mesas dotting the horizon. Jax noticed the conversation had dried up after the mention of the abduction.

Passing the mesas, Bluey slowed down, allowing them to read a road sign: 'For the next 120 km, you are in the land of the Min Min Light – This unsolved modern mystery is a light that at times follows travellers for long distances – it has been approached but never identified.'

"Remarkable," Jax exclaimed. "Looks like we're in the right place."

Exiting the taxi at the Australia Hotel, they stepped into the hallway, where Jax paused to look at the extensive collection of Min Min light paraphernalia.

"The Min Min lights thing must be the town's big attraction," Doc remarked.

Jax grinned. "That and the Bourke and Wills waterhole."

"Of course. I'd drive over two thousand kilometres to dip my toe in the waterhole," Doc said.

Jax rolled her eyes at his sarcastic comment. They proceeded to the reception to check in.

Later, Jax entered the main bar of the hotel. It was a classic bush pub, complete with a pool table. Sitting at the bar, she watched four boisterous cowboys playing pool. The bartender, clearing tables, looked visibly annoyed by the cowboys' noise. He moved behind the bar, keeping an eye on them as he approached Jax.

"Welcome to Boulia, miss. What can I get you?"

"I'll have a Four X thanks. Guess I should be calling it a four 'X-files' in this town," Jax joked.

As the bartender poured the beer, the cowboys subtly nudged each other, glancing at Jax. Handing her the drink, he said, "Sure should, with another disappearance and all."

She paid, then savoured her drink, its refreshing quality eliciting a broad, contented smile.

"So there have been others, huh?"

"Sure ... you know, over the years. The wife of the abducted scientist is still in town. She ain't going nowhere until she gets some answers, I reckon."

One of the cowboys called out to Jax, "Hey missy, feel like playin'?"

"No thanks. Don't play pool."

The cowboy chuckled devilishly, "Weren't talkin' 'bout pool." The laughter of his companions filled the air. The bartender, displeased with their behaviour, leaned in closer to Jax, his voice low. "I wouldn't entertain them, miss. They're not from around here; they're trouble just waiting to happen."

The cowboy who had made the remark swaggered over to the bar, flaunting his bravado. He halted, pointing his pool cue threateningly at the bartender. "I think you should mind your own business, fella."

"Don't need any trouble around here, son. Now, stand down," the bartender warned.

The cowboy edged the cue closer until it grazed the bartender's forehead, leaving a blue chalk mark. The bartender nonchalantly swept the cue aside and declared sternly, "Any more from you, son, and I'll be calling the cops."

"Ooo, I'm frightened ... hey, no trouble. I just want to play with this little city black gin here."

Jax locked eyes with the cowboy. "I'm just going to ignore you said that."

In the midst of the tense standoff between Jax and the cowboy, Doc sauntered in, clad in bush attire. He quickly assessed the situation and positioned himself beside Jax, requesting from the bartender, "I'll have a schooner of Four X, thanks, mate."

The cowboy appeared astounded by Doc. "Well, check this out, we've got Crocodile Chow Mein. This ain't New South Wales, boy ... we don't serve schooners in Queensland, actually ... we don't serve Cooners like her or slopes like you either."

Doc received his beer, indulged in a lengthy sip, and then exhaled a refreshed sigh, punctuated by a contented burp. He wiped his mouth with the back of his hand and gestured to the bartender. "Mate, can I have a set of darts for the board?"

Still being eyed-off by the cowboy with the pool cue in hand, Jax said, "How about you go and play pool with your mates and leave us in peace?"

The bartender handed Doc three darts. "Thanks, mate," Doc acknowledged.

Abruptly, the cowboy seized Jax by the hair. Doc responded swiftly, launching a dart into the toe of the cowboy's boot. The cowboy instantly released Jax, hoisted his foot, and exclaimed while hopping about, "Ugh! You!"

Doc clapped him on the shoulder. "Sorry mate, it just slipped."

The cowboy hoisted the cue, poised to strike Doc, but in a blur, Doc unleashed a barrage of Kung Fu moves that floored him. He spun and fired the remaining two darts at the other cowboys. One dart fastened a cowboy's hand to the pool table's rim, and the other struck the third cowboy's knee.

CHAPTER
TWO

The bartender, visibly thrilled, grabbed a cricket bat from under the bar, itching to join the fight. Jax stood, arms folded, eyeing the final cowboy, a sizable bearded giant. The brute lunged at Doc with a haymaker, which Doc effortlessly evaded and retaliated with a blow that fractured the man's nose. As Doc prepared to deliver a karate kick, the giant, clutching his bleeding nose, pleaded, "No more, no more ... you're too good for us, mate."

The first cowboy extracted the dart from his boot and returned it to Doc. "Had you scoped out all wrong, blue. Good stuff."

The four cowboys, now respectful of Doc's combative skills, gave him thumbs up as they exited the bar.

Once they'd gone, the bartender, shaking his head, remarked, "Queenslanders, they make you laugh ... Mate, you've just carved your name into local legend. Those blokes will be regaling cow-punchers in taverns across Queensland for the next thirty years about how you single-handedly bested all four of them ... They thought they were tangling with bloody Bruce Lee!"

Jax and Doc shared a chuckle. Jax's perception of Doc had certainly shifted after that display.

"Close," Jax commented, "his name is Doc Lee."

"Serious? Well, Doc Lee, you're destined to become as renowned as Bourke and Wills. Anyway, you two have earned a drink on the house."

Jax carefully dabbed at a small scratch on Doc's forehead, catching a trickle of blood. Their eyes met, and for a second, there was this kind of spark, like they both felt something more. Then Jax, getting what was happening, changed the vibe. "Time for the news?"

The bartender pointed the remote at the wall-mounted TV, and it lit up right as NewsLine started.

Jax was all smiles. "Here we go, Doc. My first story. Fingers crossed."

Her face dropped when the news anchor didn't mention her story. "You can turn it off. Looks like it didn't make the cut," she said, sounding bummed out.

Doc put his hands on her shoulders, looking right into her eyes. "Didn't you say you gotta give them a three-minute story every month?"

"Yeah, so?"

"So, they'll probably pick the coolest story you hand in, right?"

Jax, a bit annoyed, echoed, "Yeah, so?"

"Let's just focus on what we're here to do."

She gave a small, accepting smile. "Yeah, okay. Cheers to that. And hey, maybe you should keep those darts? You're pretty good with them."

The bartender laughed. "Keep 'em, Doc. They're my gift to you."

"Is the scientist's wife here?" asked Jax.

"Mrs Sagan? Yeah, she's around. Doesn't look like she's going anywhere soon."

"I want to talk to her."

"That might not be the best idea."

Doc asked, "Why not?"

Cleaning the bar, the bartender lowered his voice. "Ever since she had visitors, she's clammed up. Won't talk to anyone about it." He leaned in, whispering, "Yesterday, this black helicopter lands right in the middle of town. Two guys, like from a movie, came here, went to her room for about an hour. My wife, Edna, heard Mrs Sagan crying. Then those guys just left, got back on their chopper, and took off." He leaned in even closer. "She's stayed in her room since then. All a bit how's yer father, if you ask me."

His stare got serious to make his point. Then the phone rang, breaking the moment. Jax, giggling, leaned toward Doc. "All a bit how's yer father, if you ask me," she repeated, copying the bartender's tone. "What if I try to see Mrs Sagan while you check out the town? Deal?"

"I'll bring the darts," he said, joking around and finishing his beer. He headed to the door, waving the darts and singing in a goofy way, "Here come the men in black, here come men in black, the men in black, here come the men in black…"

Jax called out, laughing, "Mate, you're such a clown, don't give up your day job."

Approaching room 17, Jax knocked on the door. Nothing but silence greeted her. She rapped on the door again, yet received no response. Just as she turned to leave, the door creaked open a fraction, revealing a wary eye peering out.

"Mrs Sagan?"

"Go away," came the sharp reply from inside. "I've got nothing to say."

"But Mrs Sagan, I'm just trying to help."

The door inched open a tad more, enough for the woman inside to see Jax. Jax glimpsed a woman in her mid-twenties, her face alarmingly red, blistered and peeling, like she had been badly sunburned or exposed to too much radiation.

"Who are you?" the woman inside challenged.

"I'm a journalist, Mrs Sagan. Name's Jax. Blimey, your face looks really sore … can I get…"

"Listen, the authorities have warned me not to talk to anyone, especially reporters. I know you mean well, but this is about my husband's life ... it's more important than your story. Got it?"

With that, she shut the door. Jax mumbled to herself, "Yep, got it ... loud and clear. Wouldn't want to be in your shoes, that's for sure." She slid her business card halfway under the door, then stood, biting her knuckle, thinking. The card disappeared inside. Smiling, she walked down the corridor, feeling oddly satisfied.

CHAPTER
THREE

Exhausted, Jax headed back to her room and collapsed onto the bed. Her mind was racing like she was flipping through a book at lightning speed. The window was open, letting in a warm breeze that made the curtains flutter. Slowly, she drifted off to sleep.

In her dream, she suddenly sat up, hearing a voice echo like it was in a huge cave, "What time will you die." She glanced at the digital clock on the bedside table, which changed from 4:06 am to 4:07.

Plasma energy seeped through the door, and manifested into a ball rotating, a metre from the floor. It slowly materialised into the ominous silhouette of a man. Paralysed with fear, Jax could only watch as the curtains billowed towards her, as if beckoning fingers. The shadowy figure floated closer, and she could see that he was an Aboriginal elder, adorned in ceremonial body and face paint. Looking down, she noticed he was wearing feathered shoes.

Then a flash of white light showed her a memory—herself as an 11-year-old in Manila, standing under an umbrella with a younger Tilly in the rain, both crying as they watched a coffin being lowered into a grave. A priest appeared, ready to give the last rites. But then the coffin tipped over, the lid fell off, and it was empty. The priest's laugh filled the air, turning sinister and creepy, his face morphing into something demonic, with red, black-rimmed eyes and sharp teeth like a vampire.

Jax woke up, gasping for air, heart pounding. There was no intruder, no moving curtains, no alarm clock. It had all been a dream—or a memory from when she was 11? Either way, she was left shaken and in cold sweat.

Doc sauntered into the Boulia Police Station and approached the unattended counter. "Hello! Anyone here?" he called out.

A burly man with substantial ginger-haired forearms and a florid face soon emerged from the back. The constable's expression conveyed an immediate distaste for outsiders. Doc removed his sunglasses and noted the constable's name on the desk, observing a striking resemblance between him, Bluey, and the bartender.

"What do you want?"

"Constable Wright," Doc began, swiftly presenting his ID, "Doctor Vincent Lee."

"Yeah, I can read."

"I have a few questions regarding the disappearance of..."

The bulky officer turned his back and started walking away. "Nup, that's a military issue, and I don't care what ID you've got." He paused and glanced back. "I reckon you and your girlfriend won't be staying long in Boulia. And I'd be wary of staging any more scenes like the one at the bar today. Around here, I lock people up for brawling."

"You can't be very effective at your job," Doc crisply countered.

"Oh? And why's that?"

"Because you let four of them escape ... G'day."

Exiting the station, not the type to let anyone push him around or treat him like he was less than anyone else, Doc felt a rush of triumph from the encounter.

Outside, he glanced down Herbert Street towards the setting sun; the sky was bathed in a stunning orange glow. Then, a sign caught his eye across the street - 'Min Min Museum'. His curiosity sparked, he decided to check it out.

Back at the bar, Jax was the only customer, nursing a beer in the softly lit room. The bartender leaned over the counter, extending his hand.

"We never really got around to introductions, John Wright. This pub's mine ... well, mine and the Mrs."

"Good to know you, John. Just call me Jax."

"Jax... that's an odd name."

"Yeah, when I was born I was as black as charcoal, so my dad, who was a white fella, reckoned I needed a scrub with Ajax to get me a shade whiter ... The name stuck."

Their laughter filled the quiet space.

"That's as funny as buggery. Your old man must've had a good sense of humour?"

"Sure did ... a good bloke too, I'm told."

"Jax, I've got to give Edna a hand for a couple of minutes. Would you mind keeping an eye on the bar for me?"

"No worries."

As he left, John called back, "Help yourself to a refill when you're ready, aye Jax?"

"Thanks, John."

Alone in the quiet bar, Jax was taking a sip of her beer when suddenly, the eerie sound of a didgeridoo filled the room. A shiver shot down her spine, and she spun around. As quickly as it had started, the music stopped, revealing an old Aboriginal man standing nearby.

Jax jumped. "Argh! You scared the life out of me. I didn't even see you come in."

"No, but you heard me. You're here about the white fella who was taken," he said, sitting down next to her.

Jax studied him closely. His face, framed by long white hair, seemed a tapestry of Dreamtime stories. His eyes had a kind of deep wisdom.

"Yes, I am. How did you know? Have we met before?" she asked.

"I am your guide ... I am of your blood."

"Right, I figured we're from the same mob ... but it feels like more than that." She caught herself, getting back on track. "So, what can you tell me about the man who was taken? What's your name?"

"You've got a lot of questions, Jannali ... Close your eyes, and let Jibbi Jib lead your vision."

A bit hesitant, she closed her eyes. The didgeridoo started again, louder this time, with the sound of clapping sticks. In her mind, she saw a road at dusk, Mrs Sagan and a man, maybe Mr Sagan, cycling together, laughing.

"It's not far now, love. Boulia's just over that hill," Mr Sagan said in an American accent. "Look, you can see the city lights ... all four of them," he joked.

"My legs are killing me. We should've driven."

Suddenly, two lights appeared ahead. The Sagans stopped, mesmerised. The lights floated above them.

"Aren't they amazing, Justine! They must be the Min Min lights!"

The lights moved away, and Daniel followed, leaving Justine behind. "Daniel, wait ... I can't keep up!" she shouted.

The lights led Daniel over a hill. Justine pedalled hard to catch up, but when she got to the top, there was only an eerie glow and Daniel's bike abandoned on the road.

"Daniel? Daniel!" Her voice shook with fear.

The Min Min lights, now three, hovered, eerily silent.

"Daniel!" she screamed, tears in her eyes. "Please, bring him back! Don't take him!"

Suddenly, she was enveloped in a blinding light. The music stopped, and Jax's eyes snapped open.

"Argh!"

Jibbi Jib looked at her seriously. "You won't find answers here, Jannali. You must journey to the den of the Min Min, the most sacred site for your people."

"Why did you call me Jannali?"

"It's your sacred name. It means moon."

Jax thought about Xiang's words, comparing her to the moon.

"Thanks, Jax," John's voice suddenly brought her back to reality.

Jax turned quickly, seeing John behind the bar. "You scared me. I was just talking to Jibbi Jib here..." She turned back, but the old man was gone.

"Who?" John looked puzzled.

Flustered, Jax faced him again, touching her forehead, doubting herself. "Jibbi Jib, an Aboriginal elder. He was right here beside me. Didn't you see him?"

John looked around. "No, love, not a soul."

CHAPTER
FOUR

Doc was examining the exhibits with the curator, Jane Wright. She was a red-headed 'greenie' in her 40s, attractive in an earthy manner. They stood before a photograph of the Min Min lights displayed on the wall.

"I had no idea there have been so many sightings of them. Have you ever seen them, Mrs Wright?" Doc inquired.

"It's Miss Wright, but please, call me Jane. Yes, over the last decade, I've probably seen them a dozen times or more."

"What do you think causes them? Feel free to get as scientific as you want, I'll understand."

"I often get asked that, and I have a standard response based on various studies. One theory is bioluminescence, possibly from insects or animals affected by fungi. Another is the Fata Morgana mirage, an optical illusion caused by light bending through temperature layers. Some suggest geophysical phenomena like piezoelectricity or methane gas. However, none of these theories have been conclusively proven."

"That's a thorough and well-rehearsed answer. So, the phenomenon remains unexplained. I spoke to Constable Wright about the recent disappearance linked to the lights, but he wasn't very forthcoming."

"Ah, cousin Bob can be a bit dodgy ... much like the Min Min lights... always bobbing to dodge the issue," she said with a hint of dry humour.

"Ha! Seems like it ... But why do you think that is?"

"The lights are a major source of tourism income for Boulia. He's loath to either admit or deny their existence. Could lose him his job one way or t'other if he did ... so he bobs..."

"I see your point ... What's your take on the alleged abduction?"

Jane guided him towards a display of souvenirs, picked one up, and gave Doc a knowing look. "Well, I do need to sell a few of these every week to keep the museum running."

Jax was stepping off her bar stool to leave when Doc entered, carrying a paper bag.

"What's up, doc?" John quipped.

Doc chuckled. "Just bought enough souvenirs to last a lifetime. A beer, please, mate."

As John pulled him a beer, he remarked, "You've obviously visited Jane at the museum. She's my cousin, you know?"

"And Constable Wright is your...?"

"Brother, correct ... The Wright Brothers ... That's why," John pointed to a framed photo of a WWII Kittyhawk fighter aircraft on the far wall, "there's a Kittyhawk up there."

Doc observed the photograph.

"Oops, you've lost me ... What's a Kittyhawk got to do with it?" Jax asked.

Doc placed four pewter figurines of a miner mining opal on the bar. "The town of Kittyhawk is where the Wright brothers achieved the world's first powered flight, right?"

"Okay, now that I've had my history lesson, what did you learn from buying these figurines?"

Taking a sip of beer, Doc replied, "Ah! That's bloody terrible," he joked, enjoying the cool ale. "Nothing from John's brother ... But Jane, the museum curator, shared quite a bit ... According to Aboriginal legend, catching the Min Min lights leads to disappearance. Maybe that's what happened to Sagan. Alternatively, Sagan, a scientist from Pine Gap, was either abducted by aliens, or more plausibly ... Dr Sagan, stationed at Pine Gap, elopes with his love and they head to Boulia to marry. They think they're safe, take a bike ride, but the US authorities, unhappy with their secrets roaming free, snatch him from a chopper, the lights mistaken for Min Min lights. The US Men in Black arrive in Boulia the next day to silence Mrs Sagan. Hence Constable Wright's dismissal of me. That's my theory. How did you fare with Mrs Sagan? But before you answer, I bet you got the flick as well."

"How perceptive of you," Jax said with a self-satisfied smile.

"Elementary, my dear Jax ... Done and dusted. Ready to leave?"

"Doc?"

"Yes?"

"I'm going to nickname you 'Nothing'. Do you know why?"

Intrigued, he replied, "No, why?"

"Because nothing's impossible with you. Your theory doesn't account for Mrs Sagan's radiation burns. We're off to Alice Springs." She pulled out her phone and dialled. "Hello, Silver City air taxis? I need a pick-up ... hang on ... Bad signal." She stepped outside.

Doc downed his beer, placed the empty glass on the bar, and said to John, "She's dead serious. Another round, please, mate. Looks like a long night ahead."

Once again, they found themselves seated in the tin shed at the airport, this time engulfed in darkness, save for the faint glow of a solitary globe dangling from the rafters. Around it, thousands of moths fluttered, drawn to its light.

"Well, at least there are no flies," Doc said with a chuckle.

"No, but we could do without the moths. Doc, something's happening to me," Jax spoke solemnly.

He looked at her, misconstruing her meaning. "I know ... I think I'm feeling it too. If you want, we can..."

"Not that ... Something spiritual. I've been seeing someone."

"That's okay. There's no need to feel guilty. We can have an open relationship."

"No, not that either, stupid. Just shut up and listen. I think I had a visit from an Aboriginal spirit ... and I think it's because I've opened my mind to it for the first time. Well, Xiang opened my mind."

"I think you might be getting a little caught up in the supernatural since..."

"No, I haven't. I have to follow this, Doc. I'm being serious; it's not just some random feeling. I feel it's leading me to something."

Doc pondered for a moment, then said, "It makes sense to check out Alice Springs. Maybe you'll find your answers there?"

"The plane is coming," she said, standing up.

"Right, now you're gonna tell me you can instinctively feel it, right?"

"No, I can see it. Look, there."

Doc looked up just in time to see the landing lights of the plane as it touched down on the runway.

CHAPTER
FIVE

Alice Springs, the pulsating heart of Australia's Red Centre, stands as a town unlike any other. It's a place where the timeless Aboriginal culture weaves seamlessly into the fabric of contemporary Australian life, creating a distinct amalgamation of history and modernity. Here, the sun-baked earth converges with the vivid tones of the MacDonnell Ranges, offering a breathtaking canvas to a town abounding with adventure and enigma. Alice Springs, with its profound historical roots and untamed beauty, emerges as a genuine sanctuary in the expansive Australian outback.

A taxi arrived at the Crowne Plaza Lasseters. Jax and Doc stepped out of the cab and proceeded towards the reception.

Moments later, they were en route to their individual rooms. Doc's accommodation was adjacent to Jax's. Pausing at his door, key in hand, he joked, "Hey, wouldn't it have been more cost-effective to share a room?"

"Forget it, mate. Meet me poolside after lunch, okay?"

Her mobile rang just as she unlocked her door. Entering, she flung her small bag onto the bed and began to pace while answering, "Yes ... Mr Carter." She recoiled, momentarily pulling the phone away from her ear at his booming voice. "Yes, sir, I'm aware my budget doesn't extend to chartering planes, but I assumed ... Yes, sir ... ye s...

no ... trust me, this story is momentous..." She again retreated the phone from her ear as Carter's irate tone persisted. Simulating signal issues, she cut in, "I'm losing you, sir..." mimicking static noises with her mouth. "No ... p ...poor signal ... can't hear..." She hastily concluded the call and disdainfully flung the phone onto the bed, then strode into the bathroom. The phone rang again. From within the bathroom, she shouted, "Go to hell, Sir!" her voice saturated with frustration at her boss's demanding nature.

Beneath a cloudless sky, in the sweltering heat, Jax made her way towards the pool. It was like an oasis, a striking blue expanse surrounded by date palms and lush tropical plants, set against the red backdrop of the desert. She couldn't help but shake her head in disapproval upon noticing Doc engaged in conversation with an attractive, bikini-clad woman by the poolside. Jax claimed a chair next to them.

"Jax, this is Darli. She's a model," Doc introduced.

Peering over her sunglasses, Jax replied with a hint of sarcasm, "Of course she is ... Hi."

Darli offered a brief smile in response.

"Are you a local, Darli?" Jax inquired, casually.

"Born and raised ... But I've relocated to Adelaide. Just back to visit my mob," Darli shared.

Jax's gaze was abruptly diverted to a figure standing on the opposite side of the pool. The man bore an uncanny resemblance to Jibbi Jib, the elder she had encountered in a pub at Boulia.

"Feel like a swim?" Doc suggested, standing up and taking Darli's hand.

Leaving her towel, Jax stood and began walking towards the elderly man, as if drawn by an invisible force. Doc and Darli plunged into the pool.

As Jax neared the man, she called out just as he began to walk away, "Jibbi Jib! Wait!" She quickened her pace in pursuit.

From the pool, Doc watched Jax stride into the surrounding bush, seemingly calling out to an unseen figure. "Jax!" he yelled. "Who's she talking to? ... Come on, Darli, we should follow her."

Pushing through the bush, Jax was guided by the resonant sounds of a didgeridoo and rhythm sticks. She emerged into a clearing where a Corroboree was in full swing. Aboriginal dancers, adorned with ceremonial paint, moved energetically around a roaring fire. Their dance was harmonized by the rhythmic melody produced by a circle of musicians, among whom Jibbi Jib was seated.

As Jax cautiously approached, the night air pulsated with the primal rhythms of the Corroboree. She reached out, her hand trembling slightly, to tap Jibbi Jib's shoulder, only to gasp in utter disbelief. The figure before her, once the familiar form of Jibbi Jib, had mystifyingly transformed into an elder woman. "But how?" she breathed, her voice a mix of wonder and bewilderment.

The woman, cloaked in the enigmatic aura of the Dreamtime, merely gestured towards the dancers with a knowing look. As Jax's eyes followed, the music climaxed, its ancient beats echoing in the depths of her soul. The world around her began to shift and swirl; the fire's glow intensified, casting otherworldly shadows that danced with the flames. In a mesmerizing flash, the stark light of day was swallowed by the velvety cloak of night, transporting her into the heart of the Dreamtime.

Before her, the dancers' movements became an ethereal spectacle, their bodies weaving a story older than time. It was as if she was seeing through a veil that obscured the true essence of their dance from ordinary eyes. A hushed whisper escaped her lips, "They're re-enacting the Boulia abduction!" The revelation hit her like a thunderclap, revealing a hidden layer of reality that lay just beneath the surface of the ordinary world.

The portrayal of the symbolic abductee was mesmerising. He mimed pedalling a bicycle, and as a light emerged in the performance, he halted, dismounted, and then, with arms outstretched, was hoisted into the air by four dancers. The dancers then gracefully retreated, the music transitioning to a haunting tune, the lighting shifting to an eerie blue hue. Remarkably, the 'abductee', now without the assistance of the dancers, gently descended to the ground, landing in a spread-eagled pose.

As the music's tone altered again, a dancer, completely coated in white paint and strikingly resembling a grey alien in Jax's eyes, emerged from the shadows. The abductee slowly stood, his movements depicting confusion and shivering, as if emerging from a bewildering encounter.

Doc and Darli, having arrived, stood beside Jax, who was seated on the ground as though meditating.

Upon opening her eyes and looking up at Doc, she exclaimed, "Look at this, Doc, you won't believe it ... they're enacting the Boulia abduction story."

But when she turned her gaze back to the dancers, she found herself alone. The clearing was deserted, the captivating performance vanished, leaving her in a silent, empty space—a stark contrast to the vivid tableau she had just witnessed.

"It all vanished the moment you arrived ... I ... I..." Looking all at sea, she stood and then seized Darli by the arm. "Darli, Darli, you speak the local language, don't you?" Jax asked urgently.

"Yes," Darli replied, a hint of confusion in her voice.

"Then help me find Jibbi Jib."

An elderly woman suddenly appeared from the bushes, stepping into the clearing.

"There, there! Ask her where Jibbi Jib is. I followed him here, and he turned into her?" Jax said, pointing to the woman.

Darli glanced at Doc, her expression betraying concern that Jax might be delusional.

"Ask her!" Jax implored. "Ask her name?"

After a brief exchange in the native dialect, Darli turned back to Jax. "Her name is Tula, and she claims no knowledge of a Jibbi Jib ... but she's willing to answer your questions."

Doc looked on, puzzled. 'How would she know?' he thought.

"Good," Jax said tersely. "Ask her if I imagined the Corroboree? And the abduction story?"

Darli relayed the questions, and Tula responded with a laugh.

"She says you didn't imagine it ... you were shown the truth in the Dreamtime."

Jax, her hand pressed to her forehead as though struggling to stay conscious, barely grasped the revelation. "Where do the Min Min lights go?" she asked faintly.

Darli translated. Tula's response came with a solemn nod. "She says they go to a sacred place."

"And where is this sacred place?"

Darli paused, her knowledge precluding the need for translation. "Quiurnpa," she said softly, "The white folks call it Pine Gap ... the military has taken the lights ... the lights that carry our people's spirits to the Dreamtime."

Jax reached out, touching Tula's shoulder in a gesture of gratitude. "Thank you, Tula. Now I understand."

Turning, she began walking back towards the hotel, her mind racing with newfound insights.

Baffled and a bit irritated by her sudden departure, Doc called out after her, "Jax! Now, where are you going?"

CHAPTER SIX

Jax entered her room and collapsed onto the bed. She lay there, her gaze fixed on the ceiling. The light filtering in from outside cast a pattern on the ceiling, eerily reminiscent of the designs painted on the Aboriginal dancers at the Corroboree. She had been a part of something new yet ancient, an experience that was mystical and deeply spiritual. Closing her eyes, she surrendered to sleep, her mind still swirling with the day's revelations.

Meanwhile, in his hotel room, Doc sat engrossed in front of his laptop. The light from the screen illuminated his focused expression, reflecting off his reading glasses. His internet search had led him to a scholarly article titled 'The Earth Grid', which seemed to hold potential clues to the mysteries they were encountering.

Later, Doc and Darli found themselves in the hotel bar. They chose a table and settled in, ready to enjoy the performance of a solo artist on the small stage. The performer, a First Nations girl in her early twenties, sat poised on a stool. She skilfully played an electric guitar, her music enriched by a pre-recorded backtrack. Doc found himself captivated by her expansive vocal range. As she began the final song of her set, a hush fell over the bar, the audience drawn into the spell of her music.

There seems to be so much bad news,
Everybody's busting each other's dreams.

Don't cut me down to size when I speak my mind
I'm an outspoken woman, sure as hell not blind.

I've got my religion – peace of mind to find,
So come on now fella – let's walk the same line.

I'm a girl of the world
See it in my eyes
I'm a girl of the world, got nothing to hide

Don't try to tell me what I have to do
I've got my own mind – got my dignity too.

Life is tough enough – without being unkind
Show me you're a good man – show me that smile.

I know you want to lay me – that's what's on your mind
But I ain't no conquest – for your 'piece' of mankind.

I'm a girl of the world
See it in my eyes
I'm a girl of the world
Got nothing to hide

I'm a girl of the world mother nature's child
A girl of the world
Mother nature's child…

I can do anything — I want to do
Do it any time — think I might
I hold my life — in my own two hands
I am who I am — not what you demand!

I'm a girl of the world
See it in my eyes
I'm a girl of the world
Got nothing to hide

I'm a girl of the world
Mother nature's child
A girl of the world
Mother nature's child…

The song concluded to enthusiastic applause from Doc, Darli, and the roughly thirty other audience members. As the performer set down her guitar, Doc was taken aback to see her heading straight towards their table. Darli stood and welcomed her with a warm embrace, while Doc got to his feet.

"Doc, meet Alona, my sister," Darli introduced them.

Doc extended his hand, impressed. "Hey, you were fantastic. Now that I see you both side by side, the family resemblance is clear. Please, join us."

Darli's curiosity piqued about the last song. "That last song…"

"Girl of the World?" Alona interjected.

"Yes, did you write it?"

"I co-wrote it with a guy in Sydney, online. Did you realise it's about you?" Alona asked Darli, her smile playful.

Darli's smile mirrored her sister's. "I had my suspicions, but I also think it resonates with every girl's journey."

Alona's gaze then shifted to Doc, her expression earnest. "This girl went through a lot to succeed in her career."

Doc nodded in understanding. "I can relate to that struggle. And your song captures it beautifully. It was truly exceptional. Do you have plans to release it?"

"Soon, hopefully. We recorded it a few months ago. Darli was the one who paid for the studio time ... she's the diamond, my big sister," Alona shared with a look of gratitude towards Darli.

Asleep on her back, Jax remained motionless, a picture of deep slumber. Abruptly, the haunting sound of a didgeridoo shattered the silence, its deep tones reverberating through the room. Jax's eyes darted rapidly under her closed eyelids, her subconscious stirred by the ancestral music. The Aboriginal pattern, cast upon the ceiling from the light outside, began to creep along the wall, moving across the pillow, and finally imprinting itself upon her face. The rhythmic clicking of sticks synchronised with the didgeridoo, growing louder and more insistent.

Suddenly, her eyes flung open wide as a loud banging resonated at the door. The music ceased abruptly, plunging the room back into silence. Jax sat up, startled, her heart racing with adrenaline.

Outside, Doc's voice was clear, "Hey, it's 7 am, partner. You've been asleep for hours. Meet you in the coffee shop."

Entering the coffee shop, Jax found Doc seated at a table, absorbed in his phone, a cup of coffee in hand. He glanced up at her over his glasses, "I ordered you coffee, toast, and Vegemite."

She sat down, still processing the night's events. "Ta. I can't believe I slept so long."

Doc took off his glasses, looking a bit weary. "You needed it, I guess. Gave me a chance to dig into some research."

"I think I did some research too, in my dreams. What did you find?"

Doc put his glasses back on and began to read from his phone. "The Earth Grid. It's about a place in Australia where two opposing force fields converge, creating a gravity vortex. This neutral centre, called a Bloch Wall, is part of the radiant energy spectrum. These 'hot spots' on the Earth grid resonate at 10^{12} Hertz, a frequency that could generate a vortex in space-time. This place, a sacred site to the indigenous, is where Pine Gap, a secretive U.S base, is located. There's a similar vortex in the Bermuda Triangle."

Jax was intrigued. "That's in line with my theory, but doesn't help yours much."

Doc sighed. "Here's the thing, Jax. I applied for a job during the Eight Dragons investigation, something to help with Uni expenses. I didn't get it, so now I'm a bit strapped for cash. I can't afford to keep working with you, not like this."

Jax responded casually, "No worries, I'll pay you from my earnings and get NewsLine to cover our costs."

As they were talking, a waitress arrived with three cups of coffee and toast with Vegemite.

"Three cups?" Jax questioned, curious.

"One for you, one for me, and one for ... Ah, here she comes. Good morning, Darli."

Darli approached, looking bright and energetic. "Morning, guys. How are you feeling, Jax?"

"Still a bit wobbly ... these visions..."

"About Jibbi Jib?"

"Yes."

"Can you tell me about your first encounter with him?" Darli inquired, taking a seat.

"He just appeared in my hotel room in Boulia," Jax began, her voice tinged with a mix of wonder and bewilderment. "It was as if he entered as a sphere of energy, an orb that shimmered and pulsated. Then, almost like a mirage taking solid shape, he transformed into his physical form."

"Describe what he was wearing?" Darli prompted.

Jax recalled, "Traditional white body and face paint, a loincloth, and shoes adorned with feathers."

"Those are intathurta shoes ... He's a Kurdaitcha man. The shoes make him invisible to others and enable him to move without a sound," Darli explained.

Doc, intrigued, asked, "What exactly is a Kurdaitcha man?"

"In Indigenous Australian culture, natural death isn't recognised. Deaths are attributed to evil spirits or curses, often identified by those near death. A Kurdaitcha man is a ritual executioner sent to seek vengeance," Darli explained.

"But why would a Kurdaitcha man visit me? There hasn't been a death," Jax wondered aloud.

"He's also a shaman, a conduit to the Dreamtime. His visit might be connected to the Min Min lights being captured, possibly for study at Pine Gap," Darli suggested.

Doc, with his scientific perspective, connected the dots. "The magnetic grid anomaly at Pine Gap ... The U.S. military might be examining the Min Min lights. It could have been part of Dr Sagan's work."

"He called me Jannali," Jax added.

"The name means 'moon'," Darli informed her. "In shamanic terms, it's a name of immense power."

CHAPTER
SEVEN

A long stream of red dust trailed behind Darli's SUV as it sped along the dirt road, cutting a gun-barrel line through the flat red desert plain. Darli was at the wheel, with Doc riding shotgun and Jax nestled in the backseat. Doc was in the midst of recounting Alona's captivating performance at the casino bar to Jax when Darli decelerated the vehicle.

"There's a sign ahead," Darli interjected, her voice cutting through their conversation.

Gently braking, she brought the brown Toyota RAV4 hybrid to a stop. They all peered at the sign standing starkly against the landscape: 'US Government Military Installation of Pine Gap - Proceed no further - this is a military zone. Trespassers will be imprisoned.'

"That's a bit heavy," remarked Doc remarked dryly, his tone betraying a mix of scepticism and amusement.

Darli glanced back at her companions. "Should we go up to the gates?"

Jax leaned forward, her eyes glinting with determination. "Go for it," she said confidently.

As they crested a small rise, a high fence surrounding the base came into view.

Doc continued, his voice tinged with intrigue. "Rumour has it that Pine Gap has underground levels like Area 51 in the States. Some say there are downed UFOs and extra-terrestrial remains hidden here, though officially, it's just a satellite monitoring station."

"Yeah, right ... Why here, though? Why not use Parkes in New South Wales if it's good enough for NASA?" Darli mused.

"You've got a point there," Doc conceded.

Darli brought the car to a halt in front of the towering ten-foot-high gates. Almost on cue, a military jeep rolled up from within Pine Gap, heading towards them.

Jax chuckled from the backseat, "Well, that didn't take long."

Doc and Jax exited the vehicle, leaving Darli behind to wait. After presenting their IDs through the mesh, the security personnel unlocked the gate, guiding them onto a jeep before driving off, abandoning Darli in the SUV.

Throughout the bumpy journey towards the facility, Doc and Jax scrutinised the layout of the base. A dozen massive, white domes, like colossal golf balls, were interspersed among approximately ten principal structures of varying dimensions. Jax cast a questioning glance at Doc, who responded with a shrug, equally baffled by their function. The jeep came to a stop outside an elongated, two-storey building, where the guards escorted Jax and Doc inside.

The interior of the building was sleek yet austere, a hallmark of military establishments. They halted before an office door, instructed to wait. The guards withdrew. The door bore the inscription: Colonel Charlie Connors, Base Commanding Officer. After a brief interval, an adjutant motioned them inside, then to another office.

Colonel Connors, a distinguished American in his fifties, clad in military attire, stood behind his desk and signalled the adjutant to depart. He spoke with a southern drawl, "Doctor Lee and Miss de Loite, welcome to Pine Gap. I'm Charlie Connors ... you can call me Chuck. You Aussies are fond of nicknames, mine's inspired by the 60s TV show 'The Rifleman', featuring my namesake..." Receiving no reaction, he proceeded, "Hmm, seems that was before your time. Please, take a seat." They obliged.

Just as Jax was about to speak, Chuck gestured for silence. "I know, I know, you're eager to hear about Dr Sagan. Let me assure you, this could have been a rather mortifying predicament for us ... But, I believe the best approach to quench your curiosity is to..."

A buzzer interrupted, drawing his attention to a compact surveillance screen on his desk.

"Excuse me..." He pressed a button. The door opened, and the same adjutant ushered in a man clad in a white lab coat.

Chuck rose. "Miss de Loite and Doctor Lee, this is Dr Sagan."

Dr Sagan greeted them with a friendly nod.

Jax, bewildered, began, "But?"

Chuck interjected. "Thank you, Doctor Sagan." He nodded at the adjutant.

The adjutant acknowledged Sagan, and they left. Chuck motioned for Jax and Doc to sit once more. "As I was saying, it could have been quite embarrassing for us, yet we managed. It turns out, Dr Sagan was romantically involved with a woman in Alice Springs. They wed, and she desired to depart from Alice Springs ... I'm not implying that was her sole motivation ... but we're fairly certain she saw Dr Sagan as her opportunity to leave. When Dr Sagan declined to accompany her, she concocted an intricate abduction hoax to coerce us into relinquishing the esteemed doctor."

Suddenly, both Chuck and Doc were distracted by Jax, who had reclined in her chair, laughing heartily.

"Yeah, well, I guess you could find it amusing," Chuck said, visibly agitated by her laughter.

"Ah, Colonel," Jax said with a sigh, wiping tears from her eyes, "honestly sir ... I've never heard so much nonsense in my life. Who writes your material? I'd fire him if I were you."

Doc began chuckling as well. "She's right, Colonel. What a load of codswallop!"

Chuck stood, his face indignant, glaring at them. "I'm sorry you find the official explanation laughable ... I showed you the respect of not only introducing you to Dr Sagan but also offered an explanation of the circumstances, and you show no respect in return." He pressed a button on his desk. "I bid you both, good day."

The adjutant entered and gestured for Jax and Doc to leave. Chuck sat back in his chair, glaring with contempt. Jax remained standing, returning the stare. "I'm sorry, Colonel, no disrespect intended, but I'd consider my suggestion. There are many great writers out there. I can recommend a few if you like."

The Colonel ignored her, focusing on papers on his desk.

"Thanks for your time, Colonel," Doc said facetiously.

"So, I suppose a tour of the facility is now out of the question?" Jax joked.

Chuck snapped, "Adjutant, show the civilians out."

The tall, skinny man replied submissively, "Sir." He opened the door for Jax and Doc to leave.

CHAPTER EIGHT

Doc and Jax alighted from the same US Military jeep that had transported them into Pine Gap. The gate swung open automatically, and two guards observed them as they proceeded towards Darli's SUV.

Perched on the bonnet, Darli leapt down to welcome them. "Welcome back to Australia. How was America?"

"Glad to be back; it wasn't particularly hospitable there," Doc answered.

Jax, seizing the opportunity for a final quip, lobbed a sarcastic comment, audible to the gate guards. "Don't worry, we're on our way out ... we can tell when we're not welcome on our own country."

"So, did we achieve anything?" Darli asked.

"Don't suppose we really thought we would, right?" Jax replied, her tone tinged with despondency.

"You'd have to check with Mrs Sagan on that," Doc chimed in.

They settled into the SUV and departed.

A day later, Jax and Doc strolled from Sydney's domestic arrival terminal, heading towards the taxi rank.

Seated in the backseat, Jax engaged in conversation with Doc, who occupied the front. "Well, it's back to the grind of job hunting for me tomorrow."

"Reflect on what you've gained from this venture; a set of darts ... and those Boulia trinkets?"

"Oh, I handed them all to Darli for her community."

"That was a commendable gesture, Doc ... perhaps you'll earn some humanitarian accolade for it ... They really need Boulia souvenirs in Alice Springs," Jax remarked with a touch of sarcasm.

"I think the kids will appreciate the darts. But hey, Jax, there's this one thing from Boulia that's still puzzling me."

"Yeah, what's that?"

"When a fly lands on a ceiling, does it loop the loop to land upside down, or does it perform a barrel roll?"

"Hey..."

"Yeah?"

As the taxi merged onto the Southern Cross Expressway heading towards the city.

"What's your nickname?"

"Mine? ... um..."

"Come on, you can think of one," she urged.

"Alright ... so nothing's impossible. That just so random, Jax."

"Not as random as a fly landing on the ceiling."

Doc closed the cab door and went to the back passenger-side window. "Hey ... it's been great, dead set. I'd do it again in a heartbeat. I'll email you my conclusion for your story."

Jax leaned out of the window and punched him in the bicep.

"Hey, what's that for?" he complained.

"For nothing ... something to remember me by."

Quick as a flash, he caught her off guard with a parting peck on the lips. He ambled off towards his apartment block, turned, and gave her a thumbs up. "Later."

Jax was stunned by the kiss. She touched her lips with her fingers, feeling that odd sensation again. Then, her mood shifted, she retreated into the cab, and it drove away.

Lights resembling vehicle headlights pierced the outback's nocturnal landscape, surging past the speed limit. A police siren's wail echoed, emanating from a car in hot pursuit. The speeding lights briefly crested a hill—the same hill Dr Sagan had once ascended in his quest to unravel the mystery of the Min Min lights.

Abruptly, the duo of lights transformed into a trio, eerily hovering as if belonging to a helicopter. The wailing of the police siren intensified. Then, with a sudden jolt, the three lights veered to the left, paused momentarily, and one light descended onto the road. The remaining pair disappeared in a dazzling burst of light. The police vehicle came to a halt atop the rise, its lights intermittently casting bright blue flashes. The driver's side door swung open, and a burly man stepped out.

Constable Wright stood immobilized, his gaze fixed on an astonishing sight illuminated by his headlights. In the middle of the road stood Dr Sagan, stark naked and shivering.

A fist knocked on the door of room 17. The door creaked ajar, allowing Mrs Sagan just enough space to peer out. Recognising the figure outside, she threw the door wide open and, overwhelmed with emotion, wrapped her blanket-clad husband in a tearful embrace.

"Oh, Daniel ... it's truly you."

"Yes, Justine ... it's me, all right."

Behind Sagan, Constable Wright discreetly withdrew, leaving the couple to their reunion. In the hallway, John Wright and his niece Jane awaited him. Jane, tears streaming down her cheeks in joy for Mrs Sagan, found solace in Big Bob's comforting arm around her shoulders, his large frame overshadowing her. Silently, the trio made their way down the hotel corridor.

CHAPTER NINE

Carter was at his desk, concluding a phone call. "Good, yes, just email it to me ... much obliged ... thank you. Yes, I'll definitely do that. Okay, bye now." He hung up just as a knock came at the door. "Come in," he beckoned.

The door opened, and Jax entered, looking very humble.

"Yes, you ... you might well skulk into my office after the way you spoke to me on the phone from Alice Springs ... Not to mention your expenses! Sit down ... damn it."

"Sir," she began tentatively, bracing herself for more rebuke.

"When I assigned you the Next Files, young lady, I don't remember authorising you to berate a US Military Colonel or to infiltrate a clandestine US military base..."

"But sir ... I can expl—"

He interrupted her. "Explain! Nothing could justify your total lack of discipline. And speaking of nothing, you're fortunate that 'nothing' did explain ... By the way, he wants you to call him after I've finished dressing you down."

Jax, puzzled, queried, "Nothing? You mean Doc ... but how? Why?"

"Yes, indeed. You don't think I'd let my old friend's daughter go gallivanting around the countryside chasing phantoms and extraterrestrials without knowing who she's in league with do you? ... Don't underestimate me, young lady."

"After you rejected the Eight Dragons story, I just—"

"Who said I rejected it?"

"Well, it wasn't featured on the show, and I—"

"Listen, de Loite ... I have the final say here, unless someone higher up has a different idea ... So don't jump to conclusions, never try to second guess me. Now, regarding your story... 'Min Min', if I recall correctly..." He settled back into his chair and glanced at his computer screen.

"Yes, Sir ... 'Min Min'..."

"Well, it lacks a conclusion ... What good is that to anyone? Come here..." He stood and beckoned Jax to join him at the window. "Look out there, de Loite." He playfully tugged her hair, making her lean out the window. "See those people down there in the street ... driving their cars, walking the footpath, going about their lives?"

She peered down the ten floors nervously, "Y... Yes, Sir."

"Those are the people you are trying to inform." He pulled her back inside and held her shoulders, looking earnestly into her eyes. "They need a beginning, a middle, and an end to a story ... You got that?"

"Yes, sir ... but."

"No buts, sit down."

They both settled back into their seats. He looked more relaxed now, while Jax still had that nervous flutter in her chest, like a trapped bird desperate to break free.

"From the moment I could talk, I was ordered to listen ... Do you know those words, de Loite?"

"No, Sir."

"Think about them. What are they saying to you?"

"Um, like ... a little girl should be seen and not heard?" She said though squinted eyes.

"Great words, aren't they?"

"Yes ... well, it depends—"

"One day, listen to the whole song. It's 'Father and Son' by Cat Stevens. It might be from an old bastard's generation, but what he said in the 60s is still totally relevant today." He swivelled his computer screen to face her. "What do you see, de Loite?"

She stared at the screen, her eyes wide. "It's Doctor Sagan with his wife ... they're together!" she exclaimed excitedly.

"Now you have an ending, girl. Little girls should always be seen and heard! That's what the song is saying ... and that's why it is still relevant. Both of your stories will be next Friday's feature show ... A special ... and I've arranged a better budget and a retainer for Doc."

She nearly leapt across the desk to hug him. "Oh, thank you, thank you. Do I get a bigger office?"

"No, not yet the closet is still yours for the time being ... Now get out of here and finish that story ... You've got a deadline to meet, girl."

Jax couldn't have been happier. She headed for the door but stopped at his call.

"Oh, and de Loite?"

She turned back. "Yes, Sir?"

"Your dad would be seriously proud of you."

A tear of joy trickled down her cheek. Once she closed the door, Carter finally managed to crack a smile.

Standing outside Carter's office, Jax clasped her chest, her heart swelling with elation at the outcome. Tilly, beaming, approached her. "Wicked ... Absolutely wicked, girl ... You've got a special! The other producers are green with envy," she laughed. "Your dad would be so proud." She draped an arm around Jax's shoulders, guiding her down the corridor towards the Next Files office. "So, what's your take on my mate, Doc? Caught your fancy, has he? He's quite the catch, you know."

Halting, Jax playfully swatted Tilly's shoulder. "You doubling as a matchmaker now?" She opened her office door to find Doc perched at her desk, holding his phone for her to see. Surprised by his presence, she accepted the phone, scrutinising the photograph displayed. Her expression transformed into one of sheer astonishment. "But?"

"Behold Martin and Daniel Sagan ... identical twins ... Puts things into perspective, right? Hey ... remember, nothing's impossible," Doc remarked with a wink.

Jax grinned, settling onto the edge of her desk. "So, Colonel Chuck played a fast one on us, huh? I'll be damned."

In the days following her exclusive phone interview with Mr and Mrs Sagan, Jax felt increasingly sure of one thing: Daniel Sagan had been abducted, even though he couldn't remember any of it. Who or what took him was still a big question mark, but Jax had this gut feeling that the Min Min lights were somehow involved, possibly whisking him away to and from the Dreamtime.

CHAPTER
TEN

The week after the broadcast of her special, Jax was in her office, basking in the glowing reviews. Her phone rang, and shortly afterwards, she found herself heading to Des Carter's office. On her way, she exchanged a friendly wave with Tilly. Stopping briefly at Carter's door, Jax inhaled deeply before entering.

Carter was absorbed in a document on his desk.

"Ah, de Loite, take a seat. Your special was a hit—high ratings, and the suits upstairs are ecstatic. It's been ages since they've been this pleased. They're proposing a new show, 'The Next Files'."

Jax's eyes lit up. "Serious? That's incredible!"

"I said no…"

Her bubble burst, and she slumped in her chair.

"I meant, I said no to them altering it. I want it to remain true to what you've created, de Ville. They wanted to bring in big-name producers and writers, but I refused. The show's appeal is all due to you."

Jax exhaled, relieved. "That's a relief. It's too easy to lose control of something successful."

"Exactly. I've witnessed too many shows decline because the original creators were sidelined by executives. These executives are good at networking, not nurturing creative talent. Maintain the viewership, and you're set. Got it?"

"Crystal clear, Sir."

"I'm allocating you a post-production team. You'll write and supervise filming. Janet Holmes will be your line producer. She's top-notch and creative, so she'll handle the production side of things. If it's not a fit, we can switch, but her experience will be invaluable for you."

"Understood, Sir."

"Remember, you're in charge. Gain Janet's respect. You've already got her attention with the special, now earn her regard. Maybe start by inviting her out for a drink, sooner rather than later."

Jax stood, reinvigorated. "I'm on it, Sir. Thanks for this opportunity. I won't let you down."

"There's more ... I was the editor at Eco Magazine in Manila. I knew your dad when he was a leading journalist there ... His disappearance was a shock. After losing your mum and then Henry ... it hit me hard. I relocated to Sydney afterwards. I've always thought his story would be gripping. When you joined NewsLine, I arranged for Tilly to come here. She raised you in Manila, and I wanted her close."

Jax began to speak, but Carter signalled for her to hold off. "It may seem orchestrated, but we didn't want to interfere too much."

Jax nodded, understanding.

"Just focus on 'The Next Files'. Deal with your family matters quietly. The clues will emerge in time. And talk to Tilly about your dad's diary."

Jax left Carter's office with a thankful smile, grateful for his support and guidance.

Jax walked along the corridor until she reached the door marked 'Janet Holmes – Producer.' She knocked and pushed the door open. Inside, Janet was in the middle of a production meeting with four staff members. Jax was caught off guard when Janet actually looked up and gave her a smile – something new for her.

"Hey Janet, sorry to just pop in, but you got any time to grab lunch at the pub today?"

"Sure, how about 1 pm?"

Jax quickly said her goodbyes and headed out to track down Tilly. She tried the canteen first, but Tilly had already left for her place nearby. A quick glance at her phone showed it was only 10 am. Plenty of time to catch up with Tilly and still make it for lunch with Janet, with the afternoon left for digging into 'The Next Files'.

Parking outside Tilly's terrace house, Jax hit the doorbell, fingers crossed Tilly was home. Soon enough, the door swung open.

"Jax?"

"Tilly, thank goodness you're in. We need to chat."

"Come on in. Just got back," Tilly said, leading her through to the sunroom.

"I texted you..." Jax mentioned.

"My phone died," Tilly replied, sounding a bit sorry. "These days are crazy. Up by 4, start work at 6. It's not just about looking after you and Digger anymore. Speaking of him, heard anything?"

"Nah, still no news."

Settling in the sunroom, Tilly gestured for Jax to take a seat. "So, what's up?"

Jax paused before diving in. "Des Carter brought up a diary, Tilly."

Tilly, sinking into her chair, chewed her lip. "Guess you're wondering why I didn't mention it before."

"It's fine, Tilly. I can't get upset with you, you're practically my mum."

"Well, truth be told, I only got it two weeks back. With your busy schedule, I couldn't find the right time ... plus I knew it would be a big deal for you and didn't want to distract you, honey."

"I get it. But how'd you end up with it?"

"My cousin, who moved here from the Philippines, brought it with him. I helped settle him in. He's from Mindanao."

Jax looked puzzled. "I thought you were from Visayas."

"No, I'm from a small village in Misamis Occidental, near where your dad went missing. It was big news there. My cousin Jimenez knew about our connection. The search team only found some of your dad's stuff. An officer friend of Jimenez's had the diary. Jimenez couldn't get it then, but about six months ago, when the officer needed cash, I sent Jimenez money to buy the diary and come to Australia. Just give me a moment, I'll fetch it for you. Why don't you make yourself some coffee?"

While Tilly went to get the diary, Jax headed to the kitchen to start the coffee maker. As the coffee began to brew, the front door swung open and footsteps echoed towards the kitchen. Jax spun around, surprised to see Doc walking in. "Doc?" she blurted out.

"Hey, Jax. What brings you here?"

"I could ask you the same."

"I live here."

Jax, stunned, replied, "You live with Tilly?"

"Yeah, we're related ... distant relatives, but still family."

"Why didn't you or she...?"

"Tell you? I guess it just never came up."

Jax slumped into the nearest chair, her mind racing. It dawned on her that Carter, Tilly, and Doc were somehow all intertwined in a plot that seemed to revolve around her life. "I don't get it."

CHAPTER ELEVEN

Doc, pouring himself a cup of coffee, looked over at Jax. "Want some?"

"Yeah, sure. I made it, after all," Jax replied, a playful edge in her voice.

"Right, grab a mug from the dishwasher." He headed towards the sunroom, leaving Jax slightly amused and shaking her head. "You'd be a terrible flatmate, mate."

Just then, Tilly reappeared, holding out a sealed package to Jax. "Here it is, hon. Still unopened."

Jax, with a mix of curiosity and mild frustration, asked, "Why didn't you tell me you're related to Doc? And that you two live together?"

Tilly gave a casual shrug. "Didn't think it mattered much." She fetched two mugs from the dishwasher, quickly filled them with coffee, and handed one to Jax. They moved into the sunroom where Doc was, glued to his phone.

Without looking up, he quipped, "Guess I don't need to job hunt anymore, right, boss?"

Jax, pointing to herself, responded in mock surprise, "Boss?"

"Yes, you're my boss," he looked up from his phone and gave them both the devilish look Jax was beginning to recognise whenever he was being frivolous.

"I guess I am," Jax conceded with a smile.

"So, what's the next file?" Doc asked.

"I'm sifting through them. Most are either closed cases or too old. I've shortlisted a few interesting ones."

"Care to share?" Doc asked, still grinning.

"I'll send them to your work email once it's set up."

"I could use my personal email..."

"No, we need it secure. Can't risk any leaks."

"Fair enough."

Jax stood up, checking her watch. "I need to run. Got a production meeting at 1."

"Should I be there?" Doc asked.

"Nope, you're all about fieldwork. Tilly, thanks for the diary. And please, let Jimenez know I'm grateful. Just tell me what I owe."

"Don't worry about it, hon. Jimenez is just glad you have it," Tilly replied, her smile as comforting as always. She escorted Jax to the door. "Drop by whenever. You're always welcome, hon."

Jax was lucky to snag a parking spot not too far from The Clock Hotel. Given the time of day, she was pretty relieved to find any space at all. A quick walk later, she reached The Clock's main bar right on time, just as Janet arrived.

As they grabbed a couple of beers, another stroke of luck came their way. Janet spotted a pair of patrons leaving a table in the beer garden. They quickly nabbed the now-free spot, settling down under a large umbrella. "Ah, what a relief to just sit and chill. It's been a crazy, scorching day. Cheers," Janet sighed, raising her glass.

They both took a refreshing sip of their cold beers.

"Don't stress about me stepping on your toes as the line producer for 'The Next Files'," Janet reassured Jax. "I'm here to back your vision and manage the production stuff. That's my forte."

Jax was open. "I was kinda worried you'd have an issue with someone as young as me being in charge."

Janet laughed. "Your age doesn't bother me. From what I've seen and what Carter's told me about your family, you've got a knack for compelling storytelling."

Jax shared her ideas. "I want this show to feel new and cool, not like some old-school documentary. We're talking slick graphics, catchy tunes, and keeping it mysterious."

Janet suggested, "Like a modern, doco-style X-Files? But if you've got other ideas..."

"I'll brainstorm something. Give me a day to put together a concept that fits the vibe I'm after," Jax proposed.

"Great. The more cutting-edge, the better. Especially with all the competition from streaming services, that's what execs want," Janet mused.

Jax really felt like she clicked with Janet. It was a nice change to meet someone real in the often fake world of TV. If 'The Next Files' turned into a big hit, it would mean steady work for them, which was great in their line of work. But Jax knew this success could also bring the danger of people just pretending to get along, something pretty common in TV.

Curious to see how genuine Janet really was, Jax put her to the test. "What do you think of the first two stories we did?"

Janet didn't hold back. "Well, they could've been a bit more credible."

"Like how?"

"For instance, the ghost in 'Eight Dragons' could've been spookier. Enhancing the sound design, like contrasting the rat noises with the ghost's appearance, would have added depth. And for 'Min Min,' viewers probably expected to see the lights or something extra-terrestrial."

"So, jazz up the stories a bit? But wouldn't that compromise the truth?" Jax wondered, a bit uneasy.

Janet pondered for a moment. "It's a balancing act. In the moment, the fear and suspense are real. But when it's on TV, we need to bring that feeling to life again."

Jax agreed, "I get what you're saying. So, do you think that old saying 'never let the truth get in the way of a good story' fits here?"

Janet shook her head. "No, that's not it. We've got to stick to the truth or we risk losing our credibility. What I mean is, we need to keep it engaging and entertaining for the audience."

Jax smiled, "That's a great perspective, Janet. I think we're going to work well together.

Janet agreed, and Jax felt confident about their collaboration.

It had been a productive day for Jax. By the time she returned to the office after a lengthy lunch with Janet, most of the staff had already left. As she passed Carter's office, she noticed his door ajar and peeked inside. He was at his desk, focused on his computer monitor. Jax waved the diary she had retrieved. "Got Dad's diary," she announced.

Carter glanced up. "Oh, good. That should make for fascinating reading. Did you catch up with Janet?"

"All good, got on like a house on fire."

"Excellent. Finishing up for the day?"

"Nope, I've got Dad's diary to dive into and a decision to make on the next 'Next File'."

"Love the dedication... reminds me of someone."

CHAPTER
TWELVE

Jax entered her office and flopped into her chair. She was just opening the package containing her father's diary when the phone rang. It was Doc.

"Hey, I meant to ask, a friend's band is playing at the Friend in Hand Pub tonight. Wanna come?"

"This isn't a ploy to get me to watch you playing darts again, is it?" she joked.

"No need to show off anymore," Doc replied with mock pride.

"What style of music?"

"Progressive rock, like Gilmour…"

"David Gilmour?"

"Is there any other?"

"If Gilmour is playing, I'll be there," she teased.

"Like Gilmour, not Gilmour himself."

"You mean like Pink Floyd."

"Yes."

"Not Yes, they're more keyboard-based," Jax teased.

"Who?"

"The Who aren't prog rock."

"Jax?"

"Yes, Doc?"

"The Friend in Hand at 9, okay?"

"If I'm there, I'm there."

"Okay, Jax, I'll leave your name on the door."

"Thanks for the invite, Doc."

"And don't forget the 'Next Files' stuff. I'm all set up now."

"I won't forget." After hanging up the phone, Jax's first move was to Google 'The Friend in Hand.' She discovered 'The Time Benders' were set to play at 9 pm, a name that resonated well with a prog rock band. With a nod of approval, she turned her attention to the more pressing matter at hand—the package containing her father's diary.

To Jax, unwrapping this package was like opening a sacred relic—the Holy Grail of her father's mysterious past. This diary held the potential to shed light on the unanswered questions that had haunted her for years. Her mind drifted back to that solemn day in Manila, standing next to Tilly at a graveside, watching an empty coffin being lowered into the ground. The hollowness of the ceremony, with a priest reading last rites over an empty casket, had left a void in her heart. There had been no sense of closure, no final goodbye. Now, clutching the diary, Jax hoped to fill that void, to find some semblance of peace.

Her hands trembled slightly as she carefully peeled away the paper wrapping, revealing a nine-by-six-inch box. Her heart pounded with a mix of dread and anticipation. Gently lifting the lid, she was greeted by the sight of a rugged, dark green book. On the inside front page, in a familiar hand, was written 'Diary 4.' Jax paused for a moment, gathering her thoughts, before turning to the first page. As she began to read, she felt as though she was embarking on a journey that might finally provide the closure she had been seeking for so long.

Diary Entry by Professor Henry de Ville

1996: Today, after returning from an expedition in the Daintree Forest in North Queensland, I find myself irrevocably changed. As a Filipino paleopsychologist and journalist, I've unexpectedly fallen deeply in love with Cindy Green, a remarkable First Nations Australian archaeologist. Our connection is undeniable and profound, leading us to a significant decision: we will move to my hometown, Manila, to pursue careers as scientific journalists for Eco Magazine. Our goal is ambitious yet clear—to infuse journalism with a unique blend of scientific insight and a quest to unravel the unexplainable.

Jax quickly turned the pages to the year of her birth.

2003: Today marks a joyous occasion as our union is blessed with a daughter, whom we have named Jacqueline – 'Jax' for short. Cindy's son, Digby, affectionately known as Digger, has become an integral part of our family. Tilly, a nanny we trust implicitly, assists us in raising them here in Manila. We occasionally take the children on expeditions, introducing them to the mysterious and sometimes dangerous jungles of Southeast Asia.

2004: Our lives took a devastating turn while deep in the Mindanao jungle. Cindy, my beloved, disappeared under enigmatic circumstances. The emptiness left by her vanishing is overwhelming. It's not just her absence that torments me, but also the unresolved nature of her disappearance that plagues my thoughts. Des Carter, a Scottish-born Australian, has recently assumed the role of editor-in-chief at Eco Magazine. He brings fresh energy to the magazine, yet my dedication remains fixated on unravelling the truth behind Cindy's fate. Digger's departure to Northern Queensland to discover his own path and connect with his roots deepens our family's emotional distress. What was once a close-knit unit now feels disjointed. In moments of solitude, I ponder the distinct spirituality that seems to resonate within our family, a legacy possibly passed down from Cindy's ancestry. Despite these personal upheavals, my allegiance to Eco Magazine and the quest to find Cindy never wavers. I persist in exploring, writing, and clinging to hope—a hope that one day, answers will emerge, bringing some form of tranquillity to our fragmented existence.

Jax glanced through the final entries:

2017: This expedition for Eco Magazine took me deep into the dense heart of the jungle in Misamis Occidental. Swinging my machete to clear the thick underbrush, I felt every inch the archaeologist explorer I once was. Beside me, guiding me through this untamed wilderness, was my reliable guide, Ito Santos.

We battled through the dense foliage and were suddenly stopped in our tracks by a monumental discovery: a towering wall of intricately carved stone blocks. I paused, taking off my hat to wipe the sweat from my brow, realising we had stumbled upon the megalithic remains of a lost civilization—possibly that of the Aztec Indians.

Ito, checking his Magellan GPS, marked our precise location. A sudden flash of colour and movement in the jungle caught our attention. I sensed Ito's unease—the area was steeped in local myths and legends about spirits. Finding an overgrown opening in the wall, we entered and looked up to discover a pyramid. Overwhelmed with excitement, I quickly took out my camera to document this ground-breaking discovery. My theory was that in the 16th century, Spanish ships had brought Aztec slaves from Mexico to the Philippines, and many had escaped into the jungle, continuing their rituals and customs, including the worship of Quetzalcoatl and human sacrifice.

We explored the site, walking among massive stone blocks and remnants of once grand structures. Scattered around were giant statues of birdlike beings, some still standing, others toppled, perhaps by a long-past earthquake. In a clearing, we found evidence of a recent visitor: a fresh campfire. Someone had been here recently! The feeling of unseen eyes watching us from the dark forest was palpable. Ito, clearly afraid, shared a local legend about jungle spirits, cautioning us about the perils of trespassing on sacred ground. His story only deepened my belief that the ritualistic Aztec practices had evolved into local folklore.

Suddenly, the bushes rustled. Ito was convinced it was more than just an animal. I tried to soothe him, aware of how deeply the local superstitions ran. Needing to photograph the pyramid, I gave Ito a choice: to either wait for me or continue exploring the ruins. I handed him my pistol for his peace of mind. He chose to venture further into the ruins.

While I was capturing images of bird and snake-man glyphs carved into the stone blocks, I was startled by the sound of two gunshots and a scream. Rushing towards the noise, I found Ito with a creature cornered in a secluded part of the ruins. He pointed frantically to a hole from which the creature had emerged, a weird green glow emanating from it. The creature was a young woman, her body marked with ornate designs, hissing in fear. While Ito kept watch, I peered into the hole, the strange green light reflecting in my glasses, reminiscent of a similar eerie glow I had encountered before.

CHAPTER THIRTEEN

Diary Entry: Flashback to the 2004 Expedition

That year, my beloved Cindy and I discovered a cave deep in the jungles of Mindanao, a place where the past seemed to breathe in the present. The entrance was adorned with Aztec glyphs, and an unearthly green glow emanated from within, casting an otherworldly light on the surroundings.

As we prepared to enter, fate played a cruel trick. I tripped on a vine, inadvertently triggering a boulder, bound inside a basket, to swing menacingly from a tree. Cindy's scream still haunts me. It was too late for any evasive action; the boulder struck me on the side of my head, knocking me to the ground. My vision blurred from the concussion, I was barely conscious, yet I managed to raise myself onto one elbow. What I witnessed then was surreal and horrifying.

From the cave emerged a bizarre, winged birdman-like creature. It moved with a purpose I could not understand, dragging Cindy back into the cave with an unceremonious grip. Her screams pierced the jungle air, echoing my own sense of helplessness and terror.

Bleeding from a nasty wound on my head and barely able to maintain consciousness, I called out Cindy's name, my voice a mix of desperation and disbelief. Dragging myself along the ground towards the cave, the only response was my name, echoed back in Cindy's plaintive and fading reply. It was as if the cave itself was swallowing her voice, her presence, her being.

And then, silence. Cindy was gone. The jungle around me felt oppressive, the green glow from the cave casting sinister shadows. As I lay there, my strength fading, I passed out, the image of the birdman and Cindy's terrified face the last things etched in my mind.

2017:

As I repeated her name over and over, lost in the horror of that memory, a loud shriek from the creature snapped me back to the present. I turned and managed to snap a photograph. The flash startled her; she let out a deathly cry and flew at Ito with her long, sharp claws, tearing into him like an enraged jaguar. Ito screamed and collapsed.

Spotting my pistol on the ground, I dived for it, rolled, and fired. In what seemed like slow motion, the creature simply leaned to one side, brushing the bullet aside with the back of her hand as though she had slowed its velocity. Staggering to my feet, I couldn't comprehend what I'd just seen. She turned on me. With the gun proving ineffective, I took flight into the jungle, luring her away from Ito. It worked; she pursued me, effortlessly navigating the thick vegetation.

Ito, barely conscious and bleeding badly from the creature's sharp claws, was confronted by a bizarre, winged man emerging from the hole in the ground. His body was adorned with the colourful plumage of tropical parrots—a figure akin to the 'birdman' who had abducted Cindy. Ito raised his head, horror-stricken, believing he was facing a forest spirit. The creature revealed a grotesquely ugly face, half reptilian, half bird, reminiscent of the feathered serpent god of the Aztecs, Quetzalcoatl. It grabbed Ito's leg and dragged him screaming into the darkness.

Panic-stricken, I fought my way through the jungle, vines whipping my face, tangling my limbs. Losing my slouch hat but driven by sheer terror, I kept running. The jungle fell eerily quiet, and I strained to listen for any sign of the creature. Then, a twig snapped to my left, another to my right! I realised I was surrounded. I spotted a clearing and made for it but tripped, injuring my ankle. As I knelt there, grasping my injury, I sensed imminent danger. Looking up slowly, I saw that I was encircled by a dozen of these terrifying creatures.

They began to close in, but abruptly stopped. Their ranks parted, allowing the snake-headed birdman who had captured Ito to step through and confront me. The intensity of the moment was overwhelming—I was face to face with a creature of legend, a being that defied explanation, a living embodiment of ancient myths.

The diary entry came to an abrupt end, leaving Jax enveloped in a cloud of unresolved mystery. It felt as though her father had been recording these harrowing experiences specifically for her to discover one day. The entries, while not indicating any immediate danger to his life, were deeply intriguing and only served to deepen the mystery surrounding his fate. As Jax closed the diary, she found herself with more questions than answers, each page having woven a complex tapestry of clues without a clear resolution. This unfinished narrative of her father's life only intensified her determination to uncover the truth.

Jax breezed into the Friend in Hand Pub, flashed her ID at the door, and made her way to the lounge area. The place wasn't packed, about thirty patrons scattered around. She looked for Doc but didn't see him, so she went to the bar and ordered a beer. Leaning against the bar, Jax watched two roadies setting up the band's equipment and another person busy at the sound desk. A fourth individual, handling the lighting console, dimmed the house lights.

Perched on a barstool, she took a sip of her beer and observed as the stage buzzed with anticipation. The four musicians positioned themselves, and the keyboardist started off with a Pink Floyd-esque sequence. Then, to her astonishment, the singer strolled onto the stage, guitar in tow—it was Doc. Jax nearly choked on her beer in surprise. The night was shaping up to be more interesting than she had anticipated.

The band's set concluded with the song "Upside Down," which really got the audience going.

Everybody's moaning
Yeah they're moaning 'bout the times
Trapped in their devices
Wasting lives online

Too many questions
From too many minds
They're questioning reason
Without validating rhyme

Well, you're
So mad
Getting all the spam
Taking it to dump it in the trashcan, man
You crack down
Rolling on the ground
Too much mind control
Can turn you upside-down

Shut down (upside-down)

Your world keeps spinning
But you're losing all control
Every place you look
You're gonna find another troll
Invaded by digits
You need to get away
You got to make it, baby
Gotta fight another day

Well, you're
So mad
Getting all the spam
Taking it to dump it in the trashcan, man
You crack down
Rolling on the ground
Too much mind control
Can turn you upside-down

Shut down

Upside-down

The bass player delivered a voice-over in a resonant godly voice, backed by the band's rhythmic groove.

We know that no-one ever seizes power
with the intention of relinquishing it,
power is not a means, it is an end,
one does not establish a dictatorship
in order to safeguard a revolution
one makes a revolution in order
to establish the dictatorship.
The object of persecution is persecution.
The object or torture is torture.
The object of power is power,
now you begin to understand me.

Then, the stage lights brightened as Doc launched into a blistering guitar solo, blending back into the chorus.

You're so mad
Getting all the spam
Taking it to dump it in the trashcan, man
You crack down

Rolling on the ground
Too much mind control
Can turn you upside-down

Jax clapped along with the modest crowd, genuinely impressed by the band's performance and Doc's unexpected talent. After the song, the audience responded with enthusiastic applause.

A few minutes later, Doc joined Jax at the bar.

"I didn't see that coming from you," she said with a playful tone. "Eat your heart out, David Gilmour."

Doc ordered a beer and sat next to her. "The Time Benders are just for fun—a group of us who enjoy jamming prog rock."

"You guys are pretty tight for a band that doesn't do regular gigs," Jax commented.

"Most of the guys are session musos, and a few of us played together in a school band called The Heartbeats."

"You're full of surprises, Doc Lee."

Changing the topic, Doc inquired, "So, what did you find in your father's diary? Must have been quite an emotional read."

"You could say that. Reading it felt like he was speaking directly to me."

"That's a trip," Doc commented.

"Yeah, I only wish I'd had it sooner."

"How so? Would it have changed anything?"

"It would have spared me years of confusion after his disappearance. The last entry in the diary didn't suggest he was in immediate danger, which is something, I guess."

"You think he might still be out there, alive?"

"I'm certain of it," Jax asserted confidently. "We buried an empty casket in Manila back in 2017, just like we did for my mum years before."

"That must have been rough."

"It was. There's no real closure in burying an empty box."

"Tilly mentioned it was just you, her, and a priest at your dad's funeral. What about your stepbrother?"

"Digger's always been an enigma, much like everything else in my family. He withdrew from us after Mum vanished, went back to Queensland to reconnect with his roots. I haven't heard from him since."

"Perhaps he'll see your name on the new show and reach out."

"Maybe, but Digger's a bit of a wildcard."

"Speaking of the show, have you found our next story?" Doc inquired, curiosity piqued.

"Actually, yes. We got a lead today from a village called Kampong Lobong-Lobong."

"And that is...?"

"At the base of Mount Kinabalu in Sabah, Malaysia."

Doc took a thoughtful sip of his beer. "An intriguing location. What's the case about?"

Jax's eyes sparkled with excitement. "You're going to love this ... Locals report a creature called the Langsuyar. It's said to prey on the unborn babies of pregnant women."

Doc's expression turned to one of disbelief. "You're not serious?"

She shook her head, her gaze intense. "Dead serious."

Noting Jax's fervor, Doc turned to the bartender. "Nev, I'm going to need a scotch ... better make that a double."

Catch the next adventure in **The Next Files** series:

LANGSUYAR